"I—I'm Not The Kind Of Woman Who Inspires Violent Emotions,"

Danetta stammered. "I'm old-fashioned and quiet and..."

"And exquisitely sexy," Cabe breathed as his mouth brushed softly against hers in a shocking, sweet contact. He tilted his head and searched her expression, assessing her helpless response with pure pleasure. His eyes were darker now, glittering with emotion. He framed her face in his hands and drew her mouth up under his.

"You said...the other day..." She faltered, trying to think, when all she knew was the warm whisper of his breath on her lips.

"I said that once my mouth covered yours there was no going back," he murmured.

Dear Reader:

It's October and there's no stopping our men! October's *Man of the Month* comes from the pen of Leslie Davis Guccione, whose books about the Branigan brothers have pleased countless readers. Mr. October is Jody Branigan, and you can read all about him in *Branigan's Touch*.

Coming in November is *Shiloh's Promise* by BJ James. You might remember Shiloh from his appearance in *Twice in a Lifetime*. We received so much positive feedback about this mesmerizing man that we knew he had to have his very own story—and that he'd make a perfect *Man of the Month*!

Needless to say, I think each and every Silhouette Desire is wonderful. October and November's books are guaranteed to give you hours of reading pleasure.

Enjoy!

Lucia Macro
Senior Editor

DIANA PALMER

HIS GIRL FRIDAY

SILHOUETTE *Desire*

Published by Silhouette Books New York

America's Publisher of Contemporary Romance

SILHOUETTE BOOKS
300 East 42nd St., New York, N.Y. 10017

ISBN: 0-373-05528-5

First Silhouette Books printing October 1989

All the characters in this book are fictitious. Any
resemblance to actual persons, living or dead, is
purely coincidental.

®: Trademark used under license and
registered in the United States Patent and
Trademark Office and in other countries.

Printed in the U.S.A.

Books by Diana Palmer

Silhouette Romance

Darling Enemy #254
Roomful of Roses #301
Heart of Ice #314
Passion Flower #328
Soldier of Fortune #340
After the Music #406
Champagne Girl #436
Unlikely Lover #472
Woman Hater #532
*Calhoun #580
*Justin #592
*Tyler #604
*Sutton's Way #670

Silhouette Special Edition

Heather's Song #33
The Australian #239

Silhouette Desire

The Cowboy and the Lady #12
September Morning #26
Friends and Lovers #50
Fire and Ice #80
Snow Kisses #102
Diamond Girl #110
The Rawhide Man #157
Lady Love #175
Cattleman's Choice #193
The Tender Stranger #230
Love by Proxy #252
Eye of the Tiger #271
Loveplay #289
Rawhide and Lace #306
Rage of Passion #325
Fit for a King #349
Betrayed by Love #391
Enamored #420
Reluctant Father #469
Hoodwinked #492
His Girl Friday #528

*Long, Tall Texans

Silhouette Christmas Stories 1987

"The Humbug Man"

DIANA PALMER

is a prolific romance writer who got her start as a newspaper reporter. Accustomed to the daily deadlines of a journalist, she has no problem with writer's block. In fact, she averages a book every two months. Mother of a young son, Diana met and married her husband within one week: "It was just like something from one of my books."

To Rozanne,
with thanks

One

Danetta Marist glared at the closed office door with all her might. He could just sit in there until he took root and grew into his expensive gray leather chair for all she cared. *He* never made mistakes; she did. If something was missing, then she misplaced it.

"It isn't worth putting up with you just to make car payments," she informed the closed door. "I'm a great secretary. I could get work anywhere. All I have to do is reply to ads in the paper, and prospective bosses will trample you trying to get me to work for them, Mr. Cabe I-Am-The-Greatest Ritter!"

She tucked a loose strand of curly light brown hair back into its high coiffure and her gray eyes stared daggers at the elegant wood door of his office. She twirled a pen in her slender fingers while she thought about the advantages of typing her resignation and stuffing it up his arrogant nose. Well, she wasn't apologizing to that bad-tempered ex-drill rigger, not for anything. It wasn't her fault that he got the calendar dates mixed up and went to a business meeting at the wrong restaurant and lost an important contract. Was she to blame because he couldn't read?

It was just like him to accuse her of doing it deliberately. He accused her of everything from stealing his pens to drinking his bourbon, and why she stuck with the job, she didn't know.

The pay was good, of course. And he did let her have the occasional hour off during the week to go shopping. And he wasn't really all that bad . . .

On the other hand, the office was forever full of salesmen speaking a strange language that seemed to have no relation whatsoever to English as they talked about various valves and parts of drill rigs and heavy equipment. Danetta knew how oil was removed from the ground, but the technical nature of her job was still Greek. She did know what a geologist's survey looked like, and that the work the geologists did was top secret when they were looking for new oil fields. She knew that because her cousin Jenny, with whom she roomed, worked for Cabe Ritter's father.

But despite her halting attempt to say so, Mr. Ritter's oilman father, Eugene, who seemed to spend his life looking for new ways to upset Cabe, had taken up one of her lunch hours explaining a geologist's duties, along with many other things she'd never wanted to know about the oil business. Eugene owned an oil company for which Cabe no longer worked. That defection into the oil rig equipment business was the source of most of the friction between the older Ritter and his son. Cabe had been certain that Eugene would go bust during the oil glut, but he hadn't. The old man had made money because he had super geologists on his payroll who could find things like strategic metals that he could sell to the government. It was all sort of cloak-

and-dagger, as she'd learned from her secretive cousin Jenny, but the discovery of the metals made money even when oil didn't.

Danetta did nothing quite as adventurous and secretive as seeking important geological formations. She wrote up orders, took dictation, typed letters for her impatient boss, made appointments and caught hell on a regular basis. And when friends and family asked what the Ritter Equipment Corporation made and sold she just grinned and pretended to have gone deaf. Once, with a straight face, she actually told an uncle of hers that Cabe Ritter designed and built photon torpedoes. Unfortunately the uncle wasn't a *Star Trek* fan, so things had gotten sticky for a few minutes, especially when the uncle happened to meet Cabe and remarked that he sure would like to see one of those planet-busters work.

"Can't you read, for God's sake!" Cabe Ritter broke into her thoughts as he muttered over the intercom. "Why didn't you tell me I had a chamber of commerce meeting at noon? It's ten minutes until twelve, and the restaurant where we meet is twenty minutes away and I'm the program chairman!"

With a sigh she pushed the appropriate button. "The meeting isn't today, Mr. Ritter," she said with forced pleasantness. "That's tomorrow. You're looking at the wrong date." *Again,* she added under her breath. "This is April the tenth, not the eleventh."

There was a brief pause. "Who turned the page?" the deep, slow drawl demanded.

"I guess I did," she mumbled with resignation. "God knows, I turned loose the last hurricane that hit the coast and I'm sure I cause gingivitis and tooth decay—"

"Shut up and come in here."

She picked up her pad and pen, smoothing her skirt over her full hips and straightening her white midi blouse. She was tall, but she had a perfect figure and long, sexy legs. Her thick light brown hair reached to her waist when she let it down. She looked very pretty with it left long, but she always pulled it up into a chignon while she worked and she was careful not to apply more than a touch of makeup to her face, barely highlighting her soft, pale gray eyes with shadow. Her face was a perfect oval, and its gentleness gave the skin a delicacy beyond words. She wasn't beautiful, but she was attractive, and most bosses probably would have noticed her even though she didn't draw attention to her assets.

She downplayed them because her boss was a womanizer, and she didn't want to risk her heart to him. She knew that she was vulnerable, because he'd given her a long, smoldering look last Christmas when she'd dressed up for a party with some of the other office girls in the building. He'd captured her under the mistletoe just as she was leaving, and her heart had all but beat her to death when he bent his dark head toward hers, with his pale eyes glittering on her soft mouth and no expression at all on his hard face. She knew she'd stopped breathing entirely. But to her surprise, he'd suddenly checked the downward movement of his head, muttered something under his breath and the kiss had been redirected to land on her cheek. He'd walked away with a curt "Merry Christmas." After that, he'd suddenly started calling her "Dan" instead of "Miss Marist" and treating her like a younger brother. She'd pretended not to notice, but since he'd made it so obvious that he wasn't going to make another pass at her, she'd never dressed up since. It was safer to be his younger brother.

Her parents in Missouri would have approved of her caution. He seemed to prefer blondes, and very sophisticated ones at that. He was quite openly a playboy, and that turned Danetta off completely. She'd never told him how she felt about his life-style, since it was none of her business, but she'd never want to get serious about such a man.

Anyway, she was only twenty-three to his thirty-six, and he seemed to think of her as a child because in the two years she'd worked for him, he'd never made a single real pass at her. He talked to her as if she were a younger man, about sports and sometimes even about his women. He didn't seem to notice that his bluntness made her blush; he seemed to be talking more to himself than to her anyway.

Lately he was dating a very elegant and cool blonde named Karol Sartain, and she'd settled him somewhat. He was much less restless than he'd been for the past few months, even if his temper was growing shorter by the day. Just yesterday, Danetta had caught him watching her with the oddest expression she'd ever seen. He'd looked at her as if he suddenly wished her in Siberia, and she didn't understand why.

Well, it was probably better that he disliked her. A man of his experience was hardly the perfect partner for a repressed maiden who kept a giant lizard for a pet.

She opened his office door and walked in. His sheer physical presence always took her breath away, especially combined as it was with his spectacular good looks. He was tall and muscular, a big man with an aggressive personality. He was a world-beater, and he looked it, with pale blue eyes that could burn holes in steel and thick, wavy dark hair that fell onto a broad forehead. He had thick black eyebrows over his deep-set eyes, and high cheekbones. His nose had been broken at least once, and his chin had a slight cleft and a couple of tiny scars etched into his dark complexion. But despite those slight flaws, he was devastating to look at, and women couldn't seem to resist him. He had all the charm in the world when he wanted something, and if that didn't work, he had fists like hams. He was afraid of nothing on earth. Except snakes. Danetta had never told him about her pet. She wondered if his fear ran to lizards.

Muscles rippled when he moved. He was all muscle. He'd worked on drill rigs until he started his equipment company, and he looked like a crew chief. These days he didn't work on rigs, but when he was in a really foul mood, he went out and worked it off on his father's ranch outside Tulsa. The elder Ritter had been a semipro baseball player back in the heyday of that sport, and he'd wisely invested his earnings in a small ranch and a string of filling stations in Texas and Oklahoma. With keen business sense, he'd parlayed that start into a successful oil business and his son, Cabe, had helped until he'd decided to get away from his father's well-meaning dominance and start his own company—which manufactured and sold parts for drill rigs.

He'd been at it for ten years, quite successfully, but his father annoyed him by never mentioning exactly what Cabe did for a living. In fact, by way of revenge, he liked to tell his friends that Cabe was a janitor at a local bar. Danetta hadn't understood the amazement of new clients at first when they realized whose son Cabe was—because old man Ritter was something of a legend in the oil business, and many of his cohorts bought their parts from Cabe. But now that she was in on the joke, it was alternately amusing and exasperating.

The elder Ritter had never quite approved of his son's independence. He liked running the whole show, and everyone's life that was in any way connected to his own. Just as his son did. When Eugene frequently visited Cabe at the office, he was full of helpful suggestions for Danetta. His last had been that she stop calling his son "Mr. Ritter" and concentrate on wearing clothes that emphasized her nice figure.

"You'll never catch his eye that way, you know," the old man had muttered, clearly disapproving her neat skirt and blouse.

"Mr. Ritter, I don't want to catch his eye," she'd replied. "He's not my type at all."

"You'd settle him," he continued as if she hadn't spoken, nodding his silver head as he towered over her, with eyes as pale a blue as Cabe's. "Keep him away from these party girls he takes around. He'll die of some god-awful disease, you know," he whispered conspiratorially. "He doesn't even know where those girls have been!"

At that point, Danetta had excused herself and made a dash for the rest room, where she collapsed against a wall in tears of hysterical laughter. She'd wanted so badly to tell her boss what his father had said about him, but didn't know how to bring up the subject.

Cabe's curious scowl finally caught her attention. "Well, don't just stand there, Dan, sit down," he muttered, watching her watching him. "I don't know what's gotten into you lately, but your mind's just not on your work."

Her eyebrows lifted sharply. "I beg your pardon?" she faltered, standing beside the chair across from his massive desk.

"Sit!" he said shortly.

She sat. The curt authority in that deep voice had the same effect on his male employees. He was so used to throwing out orders that he didn't have any inhibitions about doing it at restaurants, other peoples' parties—just about anywhere. Hostesses were said to sigh with relief when he left.

"No wonder your father doesn't approve of you," she muttered. "You're just like him."

"Insults are my line, not yours, kid," he reminded her. He leaned back in the chair and it squeaked alarmingly. He was no lightweight, even if it was all muscle. His pale blue eyes stared a hole through her. "You don't look very cheerful this morning. What's wrong?"

"You had two bites out of me before I got in the door, and it wasn't my fault," she replied.

"So? I have two bites out of you most mornings, don't I?" His eyes glittered with faint humor. "It goes with the job description. You cried for the first two days you worked here."

"I was scared to death of you those first two days," she recalled.

"Then you threw the desk calendar at me." He sighed. "It was nice, having a secretary who fought back. You've lasted a long time, Dan."

Maybe too long, she wanted to say. But she didn't.

"No comment?" He jerked forward in his chair with one of those lightning moves that always threw her off balance. For a big man, he was incredibly fast. "Look here, we've got to do something about my father."

She blinked at the sudden change of subject. "*We* do?"

He glared at her. "Yes, *we*. He's feeding the rumor mill again. His latest favorite bit of gossip is that I'm looking for a wife. My phone rang off the hook last night with offers from the aged eligible of Tulsa."

She grinned at his irritated expression. She could just see the spinsters getting their arrows out. "You know why, don't you?" she asked. "You changed the lock on your apartment and now he doesn't have a key that fits."

"My God, I had no privacy at all! I had to do it. He was waiting for me at the apartment last Friday night," he said, his eyes narrowing angrily. "I took Karol home with me after dinner and there he stood, sharpening his knife on a whetstone. He took one hard look at her and invited himself for coffee and a drink. He didn't go home until after midnight. Meanwhile he treated Karol to a monologue on the fine art of castrating calves, mucking out stables and assorted other disgusting subjects that made her sick. She went home.''

"Oh, I can understand that," she agreed, trying to convince herself that it didn't matter about Karol going home with him. It did irritate her, though, that she minded his careless attitude toward his conquests, when she should have been grateful that she wasn't among them. "I once heard him tell one of your women friends about the treatments you were taking for some contagious condition."

His eyes widened. "It was Vera, wasn't it? Wasn't it? My God—" he banged his fist on the desk "—that's why she left in such a hurry and without saying goodbye! The venomous old snake!" Vera, Danetta recalled, had been his steady date before Karol.

"Is that any way to talk about your father, Mr. Ritter?" she asked gently.

He gave her a tolerant stare. "Dan," he began, using the appalling nickname that he and he alone had stuck her with, "when he was in here last week, one of the kinder things he said about you was that you dressed as if you had pull at the Salvation Army surplus store."

She was so insulted that she forgot to protest the destruction of her name. "The venomous old snake!" she exclaimed.

He raised an eyebrow. "That's what I thought you said. Any ideas?"

"None that won't get you arrested," she replied. "Why is he interfering so much lately?"

He sighed, brushing a huge hand through his thick, wavy hair. "He thinks I need a wife. So he's going to find me one."

"Maybe he's just bored," she murmured thoughtfully. "You could ask your stepmother to take him on a world cruise."

His eyes hardened. "I have as little contact with my stepmother as possible," he said curtly.

"Sorry." She knew that was a sore spot with him, but she didn't know why. He was a very private man in some ways.

He shrugged. "I guess your parents are still married?"

She smiled. "Yes, sir, for thirty years last November."

"Don't call me sir," he said harshly. He broke a pencil and got to his feet, moving toward the window like a human steamroller while Danetta caught her breath at the bite in his voice. He pulled open the blinds and looked over the flat landscape of the city. "I don't want to get married. I don't want to love anyone."

She stared at his broad back incomprehensibly.

He fingered the blinds thoughtfully. "You haven't volunteered any information about Karol to my father, have you?" he asked suddenly, turning toward her.

His height was intimidating when he loomed over her that way. She shifted gracefully in the chair. "No, si—" She cleared her throat. "No, Mr. Ritter. He did all the talking. As usual."

"What did he say?"

She muffled a giggle. "That you were going to catch some god-awful disease if he didn't save you from those women." She leaned forward. "You don't know where they've been, you see."

He burst out laughing. The sound was deep and rich and pleasant, because he wasn't usually a laughing man. It took some of the age from his hard face, made his blue eyes sparkle. She smiled at him because he looked wickedly handsome when he was amused.

"So that's his angle. Maybe I can have a long talk with him about modern life."

"That will only work if you tie him up and gag him first."

"He's confiding in you lately, is that it?" He pursed his lips and studied her with that quiet scrutiny that was becoming more and more frequent. "How old are you now, Dan?"

"Twenty-three." *And if you don't stop calling me Dan, I'm going to wrap you in cellophane tape and hang you out the window,* she added silently.

"You were barely twenty-one when you came here," he recalled thoughtfully. "Gangly and nervous and painfully shy. In some ways, you're still shy."

"How kind of you to notice," she said, "now about the mail—"

"You don't date," he said as if he knew.

She crossed her long legs. "Well, no. Not a lot," she said with obvious reluctance.

His blue eyes searched hers. "Why?"

She chose her words carefully. She'd never had this kind of personal discussion with him before, and she wondered why he'd brought up the subject. Surely his father hadn't been trying to play Cupid for her? "I'm not modern enough to suit most men," she replied finally.

He perched himself on the corner of his desk and looked down at her quietly. "Modern as in sexually liberated?"

She felt her cheeks grow warm. "My parents were middle-aged when I came along, and they were and are very conventional people. I was taught that love should mean something more than sex. But I discovered that to most men, love meant a nice dinner followed by a session in bed. Nobody was willing to spend the time it would take to build a relationship, especially when there were so many women who didn't want one anyway. So I gave up evenings with unpleasant endings and brought Norman home to live with me."

He frowned. "Norman?"

"Norman, my iguana," she explained.

He paled and gave her a frankly horrified look. "Your what?"

"My iguana. He's a nice pet," she said defensively. "I got him when he was just a baby—"

"An iguana!" He looked quickly around the office as if he thought she'd put Norman in her purse and brought him to work with her. He actually shuddered. "My God, nobody has an iguana for a pet! It's a snake with legs, for heaven's sake!"

She glared at him. "He is not! In fact, he looks like a little Chinese dragon. He's an iguanid; a descendant of dinosaurs, of ancient Iguanodon. He's quiet and clean and you should see the effect he has on door-to-door salesmen! He's three feet long, although he's still just a baby," she murmured with a smile. Incredible that she'd never told him about Norman, but then, they hardly ever discussed routine things about their private lives. He didn't even know that she lived with Cousin Jenny, she supposed. She wondered if he even knew that Cousin Jenny worked for his father, or that two years ago, it was Jenny who had told her about this job so that she could apply for it.

"Why do you keep a reptile for a pet? Are you trying to grow your own prince?"

She sighed angrily. "That only works with frogs. Listen, I just keep Norman for a pet, I don't kiss him." She frowned. "Well, I used to when he was a baby—"

"Oh, God!" he burst out, shuddering. He stared at her. "No wonder you can't get dates! No sane man goes around kissing a woman who kisses iguanas!"

"There's no danger of that," she sighed to herself, unperturbed on the surface as she fought down the picture in her mind of Mr. Ritter bending her back over an arm and kissing her senseless. That was what she'd thought he was going to do at that Christmas party for one long, ecstatic second, until he came to his senses.

He got up and moved around his desk and sat down heavily. "I can see it now. One night there'll be a man in your apartment, and you'll call a press conference to explain how he got there. First you picked up your iguana and kissed it, and all of a sudden, poof! Prince Charming!" He frowned. "Or would you get a king with something as big as an iguana?"

"You'll be the first to know if it ever happens," she promised.

He lit a cigarette, grinning at her scowl. "You bought me that smokeless ashtray last Christmas."

She pushed it toward him with a loud sigh. "I suppose I did."

"I try to quit."

"I wouldn't call going overnight without cigarettes trying to quit smoking," she murmured dryly. She pushed the mail toward him, a gentle hint that she had plenty of work to do, even if he didn't.

He smiled indulgently. "I know, I'm procrastinating again. Did I ever tell you how much I hate answering mail? I'm still getting over last night," he added on a heavy sigh. "Karol wanted to go to a concert. We sat through four hours of chamber music. I hate damned string quartets. I'd rather have gone to a country and western concert, but she doesn't think fiddles are cultural."

She had a giggle.

"Why are you giggling?" he demanded. "Surely you realize that fiddles are a big part of the American folk scene, and that sure as hell is cultural!"

"To you, chili is cultural," she reminded him.

"Of course it is. It's the only American food I like. Why in God's name do you button those blouses up to your chin? Are you afraid I'll go crazy if I get a glimpse of your naked throat? And you haven't worn your hair down since Christmas."

Her eyes widened. That was the most personal thing he'd ever said to her and it shocked her. "The blouse...it's a jabot collar," she stammered.

"I don't like it. Can't you buy something with a V neck?" He glowered. "Failing that, you might try a shirt-waist dress, they button up."

"What is this fixation about the way I look?" she burst out. "My hair's wrong, you don't like my clothes, now I button them wrong...!"

"I don't know." He took a draw from the cigarette, his eyes going involuntarily to her long, elegant legs where they were crossed. The skirt came just above her knees, and he admired the fluid lines of her body with new interest. "Maybe my father's right, and I shouldn't have a secretary who dresses like a Quaker."

She stared at him. "Mr. Ritter, do you feel all right?" she asked cautiously.

He sighed half angrily, staring at her again. "I'm frustrated," he muttered, knocking an ash off his cigarette. "You try going without a woman for four months and see how you manage."

She felt her face burning, but she glanced down at her notepad and concealed it. "I've gone without a woman for twenty-three years, and it hasn't done me any harm," she informed him.

"Oh, you know what I mean," he grumbled.

Unfortunately she did. He was the bluntest man she'd ever known. He said exactly what he thought, no matter how shocking it sounded. He didn't even pull his punches with language when one of his clients or cohorts made him mad. In fact, during Danetta's first week on the job, Mr. Ritter had taken exception to a few remarks from a dissatisfied customer, and the unfortunate gentleman had come out of Mr. Ritter's office headfirst, followed by some of the foulest language Danetta had ever heard. It was a fascinating introduction to her hot-tempered, uninhibited boss.

He narrowed his blue eyes again and searched her face. "You never talk about your love life."

"I guess I could make up something," she said, trying not to look and sound as unsophisticated as he made her feel.

"I thought as much." He was watching her in an odd way. He seemed to do that a lot these days, as if he was curious about something. She wished he'd come out with it. He made her feel like an insect on a pin. "Too many nights alone can make a woman vulnerable, you know. Especially a repressed maidenly type."

"Are you trying to tell me something, Mr. Ritter?" she asked finally.

"I'm concerned about you," he said surprisingly. "Ben Meadows, my new sales manager, mentioned this morning that he'd been trying for two weeks to get a date with you, but that you froze him out." He smiled faintly, and his pale eyes became intent. "He thinks you won't go out with him because you've got a crush on me. In fact," he added with a stare that was pure speculation, "so does my father."

She couldn't help the flush that highlighted her exquisite complexion. Her heart jumped into her throat. She couldn't believe what she was hearing. "My gosh!"

He glared. "Well, you don't have to make it sound like a perversion," he said shortly. "Women do find me attractive from time to time."

"A certain type of woman, yes. Not me!"

He sat very still and she wondered if she'd finally gone too far. He didn't seem to move, but his eyes narrowed and grew cold. "Why not you?"

"That's personal."

"So it's personal. I want an answer," he said doggedly.

She took a deep breath. She couldn't lie to him, even if she might have done better to lie. "Because you're a womanizer, Mr. Ritter," she said, feeling backed into a corner. He was beginning to look dangerous, and she dropped her eyes to her lap. "I'm sorry, but I don't find that kind of man very attractive."

He took a draw from his cigarette and let out a thin cloud of smoke. His eyes grew brooding and even colder. "I suppose I asked for that. I didn't realize what kind of answer I might get." He sat up straight. "All right, Dan, you've convinced me that my father doesn't know what the hell he's talking about. Let's do the mail."

She felt guilty, but she didn't dare back down. He respected spirit. She'd learned her first week as his secretary that it was either give it back as good as he gave it out, or spend her life in tears. He didn't pull his punches, and he didn't respect anyone who did. As she soon discovered, he needed that toughness to deal with the people who frequented this office. Business was hard, and he was equal to it, even during recessions.

All the same, she had the oddest feeling that she'd wounded him. If a woman he called by a masculine nickname could wound him, that was. Sometimes it cut her to the bone when he called her Dan. He made it sound as if she were his fishing buddy or his tennis partner. He treated her that casually, and it had hurt. Maybe that had prompted her uncharacteristic outburst about his lack of morals.

She wondered why he was so promiscuous. In two years, she'd learned next to nothing about him, except about the type of woman he liked. About his feelings and thoughts, she knew nothing. She knew his mother had died ten years ago, and that his father had remarried a lady named Cynthia. Danetta knew that he spent time with them, but he never talked about them. His father did let a few things slip from time to time when he came into the office, but not enough to satisfy her growing curiosity about the enigmatic man she worked for.

He started dictating, pacing as usual, and she had to work to keep up with him. He wasn't sparing her. She felt the whip of his voice and the ice in his stare until he was finally through and let her go back to her own desk.

He was unusually silent for the rest of the day. She sent people into his office and buzzed him when he was needed on the telephone, but he didn't offer her coffee or stop to talk. At quitting time, he was out the door before she was, leaving her to close up without even a goodbye unless she counted the curt jerk of his head as he left, attaché case in hand.

Danetta watched him go with mixed feelings. Perhaps she shouldn't have opened her mouth. Now she'd really complicated things.

She covered the typewriter and the computer, got her purse and sweater, and went out to stand in line for the bus. She watched it approach indifferently, her mind still on her boss. One of these days I will kiss my iguana, she thought vengefully, and he'll turn into somebody as handsome as Robert Redford and then you'll be sorry, Mr. Ritter! And he'll buy me mink coats and diamonds and we'll live in decadent luxury...

She became aware of amused stares and realized belatedly that she was talking out loud.

"I'm a writer," she improvised. "It's a great plot, the iguana prince..."

"Yeah? The part about Robert Redford was great," an elderly woman said, grinning as she got onto the bus just ahead of Danetta. "But nobody would kiss an iguana!"

Danetta only smiled.

Two

Norman was curled up on the radiator, as usual, when Danetta got home. He opened his eyes and then closed them again, his long emerald-green body sprawled over the warm place.

"You're so enthusiastic, Norman," she sighed, pausing to rub his head and tickle his chin. He did look ferocious, she supposed, remembering Mr. Ritter's horrified expression when she'd mentioned having an iguana. But the reptile's fierce appearance was just window dressing in Norman's case. She'd carried him around and petted him since he was barely seven inches long, and she didn't find him in the least intimidating or frightening. It was hard to be afraid of a creature that liked spinach quiche and responded to a whistle. She was sure that a book she'd read on iguanas said they were stupid. It was a good thing Norman couldn't read.

She heated up some quiche for him and turned on a Beethoven sonata. When she put the quiche in a bowl with two or three fresh hibiscus petals from the florist, Norman sniffed and oozed down onto the floor. He looked like a miniature dinosaur, Danetta thought as she watched him plod to his food dish and eat hungrily. He wasn't much on regular meals. He ate about every second or third day, and he was certainly healthy enough. His tail gave her nightmares. It was terribly long and quite handsome, and she lived in fear of stepping on it. Iguanas shed their tails quite easily if they were pulled on, but Norman would never forgive her if she cost him his crowning glory.

She brooded most of the evening over Cabe Ritter's behavior. First he wanted her to dress in a more feminine way, then he accused her of having a crush on him, then he seemed to be mad because she denied it. He was the most puzzling man she'd ever known.

Finally she went to bed, leaving Norman on the radiator. It was still cool at night, and that warmth attracted him. He was so predictable. She could always find him on the radiator, on his paper in the bathroom—because he was housebroken—or in the kitchen. It was a good thing that Mr. Ritter had never come to visit her at home, she mused as she lay awake. Norman would give him fits.

She closed her eyes with determination, but she kept seeing her enigmatic boss's broad, hard face. She'd denied her attraction to him for a long time, and it was a good thing she'd learned to hide it. If she'd given herself away today when he'd made that accusation, she'd be looking for another job.

As if she'd ever have a chance with such a man, she sighed inwardly. He could have his pick of women, and did. Danetta wouldn't even be in the running. She only wondered why he'd been so irritated when she'd made that remark about his being a womanizer. Surely he didn't want her to have a crush on him! Of course not. She groaned and rolled over. She had to try to get some sleep.

The next morning, she felt as if she hadn't gotten even one hour's worth. She went to work dragging, her eyes bloodshot and dark circled. She'd dressed hurriedly in a green-and-lavender-and-brown swirled dress—a shirtwaist dress, although she hadn't really meant to. She left her hair down, too, mainly because she didn't have time to put it up after she'd overslept.

Mr. Ritter was usually a half hour later than she was. Today, of course, he was early. Mentally groaning as she tried to tiptoe into the office, she prepared herself for a lecture. He didn't say anything as it turned out, but he did give her a cold glance as she walked in, his eyes going pointedly to the clock on the office wall, which proved that she was a full ten minutes late. He was on the phone, nodding and muttering to someone on the other end of the line.

She mouthed an apology and started to take off her lightweight car coat.

"Keep it on," he called to her, covering the receiver. "Get the tape recorder and your pad and pen. We're going out to a rig to get some data about that new machine part I made for Harry Deal."

She had to grit her teeth. Harry Deal was an old-line rigger who hated women and made no secret of it. He made her feel like fish bait, and Mr. Ritter knew it. Which was probably why he was dragging her out to the rig with him, she thought miserably. He was getting even for what she'd said the day before.

"Not today," she sighed to herself. She put her coat over her arm as she got the necessary items together. "I'm just not up to Harry Deal today."

"Stop moaning," her boss snapped. He held open the office door, his cold eyes taking in every fact of her appearance. But they lingered on the soft thrust of her breasts and the sensuous curves outlined by the dress, and the coldness went out of them. The pale blue began to darken, to glitter. His jaw tautened and the arm that had been holding the door open moved, so that as she started to go through the doorway, he was suddenly blocking her way.

She looked up warily, her apprehension visible on her soft features. Close up he was devastating. That gray-and-beige sports coat clung to him lovingly, not too tight but certainly not overloose. Her eyes dropped, noting involuntarily the way his gray slacks molded the powerful muscles of his long legs. He smelled of spicy cologne, and her eyes rose again and stopped at the wide curve of his mouth above that cleft chin. She could feel the heat of his big body and it made her long to lean against him.

"Is this for my benefit?" he asked quietly, his eyes smoothing down the clingy shirtwaist dress.

Her heart bounced in her chest as her eyes met that glittery stare. "Of course not," she faltered. "I . . . was running late, and I didn't have time to put up my hair."

"I'm not talking about your hair," he replied, his voice deep and measured. His arm moved deliberately so that it brushed lazily against her shoulder, and she could feel the warmth of his breath on her temple. "Be careful," he murmured softly. "You said yourself that I was a womanizer. Wearing something that sexy might give me ideas."

Her shocked eyes were trapped in his stare. It was like electricity flowing between them for one long, staggering instant.

"I . . . didn't mean to," she stammered.

"Didn't you?" He moved his arm away and stood aside to let her pass. She managed that on legs almost too wobbly to support her. After shrugging into her coat, she went out to the car. Her face burned as she realized just how vulnerable she was to him. And he wasn't even trying. What would she do if he ever made a real pass at her?

There was a strained silence between them as he drove out of town toward one of Harry Deal's newest oil rigs. This was a derrick, because Harry was drilling for the first time on this new field on his property. He hadn't hit oil yet, but Danetta would have bet that he was going to. Harry could smell oil, and he had quite a track record.

"My father has a percentage of this exploration," Cabe said a few minutes down the road. He tapped ashes from his cigarette into the ashtray of his big gray Lincoln, glancing sideways at Danetta. "Relax, for God's sake," he snapped. "I'm not going to jump on you!"

She bit her lower lip until her teeth bruised it. "I appreciate it," she managed with forced humor.

He took a long draw from his cigarette and let out an audible sigh with the smoke. "It's all right, Dan," he said after a minute. "I don't have the right to tell you how to dress, although I guess I might have pushed you into what you're wearing today by the insulting things I said about the way you looked." He moved uncomfortably. "It's my father, damn it! I hadn't even noticed your clothes until he stuck his nose in." In fact, he hadn't really noticed Danetta that much until his father had started to point out her virtues. Now he found himself watching her all too often. Like right now. He glanced toward her and then away, his face tautening as his eyes registered once again how sexy she looked in a dress that fit properly. "That dress is . . . very flattering."

She knew her face was flaming. All at once she felt like one of the creatures on the endangered species list. She darted her eyes to the window without acknowledging the compliment. "You said your father had an interest in Mr. Deal's operation?"

He put out the cigarette. "A small percentage, yes," he replied, relieved to have the hot tension die down. The sight of her in that dress wasn't doing his self-control any good at all, and he hoped she was too green to realize that his bad temper was due to the new attraction he was feeling for her. "Eugene likes to have his finger in every pie he can find."

"I thought oil was a bad investment right now."

"The market's down, but it will come up again. Like gold, it fluctuates. But as long as it's a necessity, prices will eventually go up. Eugene and Harry Deal are smart enough to diversify. They'll make out."

"Is there a problem with the equipment you made for Mr. Deal?" she asked.

"He thinks so. I don't." He glanced at her and grinned. "I know the joker who's operating the rig for him. He's an old-line rigger and he doesn't like trying new things. He's probably put the damned part in backward or left it out altogether."

Which turned out to be exactly the case. Danetta, standing uncomfortably to one side while Cabe wrestled with an unfathomable piece of greasy equipment, saw the older man nearby turn red when the motor was turned back on and the part slid into place and worked with textbook precision.

The rig was overrun with men—muscular, rough-looking men who seemed to find Danetta, even in her light car coat, quite an attraction. There were some women in that line of work, but not in Harry Deal's crew. She felt all too conspicuous.

She was holding Cabe's jacket while he worked. Now he wiped his hands on a handkerchief that would never be white again and gave Harry Deal a speaking look.

Harry, a white-haired, short man with a big nose, glared at his rigger. "Okay, I stand corrected," he muttered. "Sam, you can explain all this to me later."

"Yes, sir," Sam grumbled. He shot Cabe a hard glare and stomped off to the other side of the rig.

"How's your dad?" he asked Cabe.

"Making money. He hopes you're going to fund him a new Rolls with this strike."

"I'm doing my best." He turned, pursing his lips at Danetta. "Still got the same secretary, I see. Not married yet, Miss Marist?"

Danetta hugged Cabe's coat to her breasts. "I did find one candidate, Mr. Deal," she replied sweetly, "but he couldn't change a tire and talk at the same time, so I gave him up."

Harry smiled unpleasantly. "Can't change your own tire?"

"I have to these days. Most men are so fastidious that they don't like getting mussed up doing those difficult jobs."

Cabe saw disaster ahead. He took Danetta by the arm and led her away from a smoldering Harry. "Let me know if you have any more problems, Harry," he called over his shoulder. "We have to get back to work."

"Thanks, Cabe," the older man said shortly and turned back to his job.

"Arrogant old dinosaur," Danetta muttered, all too aware of the biting grip Cabe had on her arm even through the thick cloth.

"You escalated things, honey," he reminded her. "Now get in there and keep quiet until I get you out of earshot." He gave her a faintly amused glance. "You've never talked back to Harry before."

"Maybe it's the smell of oil and grease that did it," she offered, smiling impishly. She felt free, now that she'd finally stood up to the old devil. Maybe working for Mr. Ritter had given her that bit of extra self-confidence. She'd had to stand up to him, and now it was getting to be second nature to stand up to other people. She'd . . . expanded emotionally, she thought.

He chuckled softly as he put her in the Lincoln, leaving his jacket in her hands as he went around and got in. He was still trying to get the grease off his big hands.

"Damned old-line riggers," he said on a heavy sigh. "Harry needs to fire that son of a—"

"Mr. Ritter!" She glared at him.

"Sorry, Miss Lily-White." He glanced at her as he started the car. "You ought to be used to my language by now."

"I ought to," she agreed. She leaned back against the cushy seat with a long sigh and closed her eyes. "Just when I think I've heard it all, you invent new words."

He chuckled softly. "Do I?" He sat watching her with the engine running, his eyes curious. He slowly turned her face toward him, with a big, grease-stained hand. The smile left his hard lips. "You're a little wildcat when you get started, aren't you?" he asked in a tone he'd never used with her before. "You didn't have that fire in the beginning. It took a few tears to bring it out, but you don't back away from anything these days, do you?" he mused. His big thumb moved to her mouth and suddenly dragged across her lips while he watched her reaction with narrowed, intent blue eyes.

The sensation that deliberate action caused shocked her. Her body went taut and hot all at once, and her breath caught audibly.

Her response was sheer delight. He'd forgotten that a woman could be that sensitive to his touch. She was innocent, not like the jaded, very sophisticated women who frequently passed through his life. Almost everything sensual was new to her. His thumb moved again and pressed against her mouth so that she could taste tobacco and the faint smell of grease on it. He felt his body tighten as her face told him exactly how much pleasure she was feeling. His blue eyes glittered into hers at a proximity that made her muscles clench.

"Did you know that your mouth was that sensitive, little one?" he asked huskily, searching her wide eyes. "That it could arouse you when a man played with it?"

She swallowed nervously, her body tingling with new sensations. "The . . . men on the rig . . ." she whispered.

"The windows are tinted," he reminded her in a slow, deep undertone. His thumb moved again with sensual pressure and he bent closer, so that the cologne scent of his big body overwhelmed her. Her scent was in his nostrils and he wanted nothing more in life than her soft mouth. Reason and sanity seemed to go out the window as he watched with masculine delight the helpless reaction of her innocence to his experience.

"Mr. Ritter . . . !" she murmured. He was overwhelming her, and she was afraid.

"Have you ever been kissed properly?" he whispered, letting his eyes drop to her parted, swollen lips. "With your mouth open under a man's lips?" he breathed, and she actually moaned. His jaw tautened. "It would be so easy. I could lower my head, just an inch or so," he drawled softly, moving closer, "and let you taste my breath. And then I could slide my hand into your hair, like this—" he drew her face up under his with the pressure of his fingers at her nape "—and I could kiss you like that. I could part your lips with my mouth and drag you against me so hard that you could feel my heart beating . . ."

She panicked at the mental pictures he was putting into her mind, and in one last burst of sanity she pushed at his chest, trying not to feel the hard warmth of hair-roughened muscles under the thin white shirt. "No! You . . . mustn't," she pleaded. "I work for you . . . !"

"Work for me," he echoed, his voice barely audible. He stared down at her soft mouth and felt his body clench with the need to take it. *Work for him.* The words echoed in his mind and he blinked and scowled down into Danetta's shocked eyes. Danetta! His head jerked up.

"My God, what am I doing?" he asked harshly. He let go of her abruptly and sat up, moving away from her to light a cigarette. He managed it with a brief fumble, which she was too shaken to see. "I'm sorry, Dan," he said stiffly. His heart was shaking him, and the tautness of his body was unexpected and disturbing. She was only a child. "That won't happen again."

He put the car swiftly into gear and pulled out onto the road without looking at her.

Danetta tore her eyes away from his hard features. She could hardly believe that had happened at all, except for the faint soreness of her mouth and her tingling scalp. No wonder women flocked around him, she thought miserably. He had an infallible technique. He'd barely touched her and yet he'd made her knees weaken. She could still taste his smoky breath in her mouth and hear the deliciously shocking things he'd said to her. She almost groaned at the fever he'd kindled and left unsatisfied. She'd wanted his hard lips to crush down on hers, to feel his arms go around her, his chest pressing roughly against her soft breasts. She wrapped her arms around her, trembling a little in the aftermath. What was wrong with him?

He was quiet all the way back to the office, keeping the radio between them. But all the while she was thinking, and wondering if he'd done it on purpose, to show her how vulnerable she was to him. Maybe it was revenge for calling him a womanizer. To show her that even she was wide open to his practiced technique. By the time they got into the underground garage, she felt sick all over, certain that he'd been trying to humiliate her.

She reached for the door handle the minute he parked the car, but his big warm hand caught hers, staying it.

"Not yet," he said quietly. His eyes searched hers in the tense silence between them. Something in her eyes made him feel guilty. "I've hurt you."

"I called you a womanizer," she reminded him, dropping her eyes to his chest. "Was that . . . why? To teach me a lesson?"

"No, it wasn't. And I got the lesson, honey," he said shortly, then sighed heavily. "I'm used to jaded, experienced women who take everything a man does for granted. I've never had any experience with shy, fascinated virgins who make it all seem new and exciting." He managed a wry smile at her blush. "Just for the record, Miss Marist, *have* you ever kissed a man with your mouth open?"

She went beet red and averted her face. "That's none of your business!"

"In other words, you haven't," he mused, chuckling gently. "All right, chicken, run for it."

"I don't need teaching!" she threw at him as she wrestled the car door open.

"Oh, but you do," he replied softly, his hand preventing her from jumping out. "You don't know what I'd give to be your teacher," he added with narrowed, glittery eyes. "But that would be disastrous for both of us. I'm too jaded and you're too pure. The best I could offer you would be a few hours in my bed, and I wouldn't insult you with that kind of proposition. You need a good, steady man to cherish you and give you children." He shrugged heavily, staring at the glowing tip of his cigarette, and for a few seconds he let down his guard. "That would require a kind of trust I can't give a woman. I don't want to be vulnerable, Dan."

"Nobody's asking you to be!" she said angrily, so embarrassed that she could hardly sit still.

He caught her eyes. "Are you vulnerable?" he asked quietly. "Was my father right? Don't you have a flaming, king-size crush on me?"

"No!" she cried.

There was a world of experience in his slow, knowing gaze. "Then why didn't you fight me?" he asked in a tone as smooth as warm honey.

She darted out of the car and into the building so fast that she could barely breathe when she reached the office. The first thing she planned to do was type out her resignation. But when she opened the door, Eugene Ritter was sitting impatiently in the waiting room, looking like a thundercloud.

"What have you done with my son?" he demanded belligerently.

Danetta stopped short, her hair disheveled, her mouth red from the hard pressure of Cabe's thumb, out of breath and almost shaking from what he'd said to her in the car.

"On second thought," Eugene murmured thoughtfully as he studied her, "what has my son been doing to you?"

Cabe came in the door behind her, looking smug and so damned arrogant that she could have thrown the typewriter at him.

"Hello, Dad," Cabe said absently. "Need something?"

Eugene stared at his son, looking for traces of lipstick probably, Cabe thought amusedly. The older man's face fell. "Not really," he said. "I wanted to know if you're coming to our anniversary party tomorrow night. Nicky's expecting you."

Nicky? Danetta had heard that name once or twice. Was it a man's name or a woman's? Probably a woman's, she thought miserably.

"I'm busy tomorrow night," Cabe said shortly. "I'm taking Karol to the ballet," he added, with a long, silent stare at Danetta's averted face.

"So that painted woman is more important to you than I am," Eugene said angrily. "And what about Cynthia? Is she going to suffer for the rest of your life because I had the audacity to marry again?''

Cabe turned on the older man, his eyes dangerous. ''She'll never be my mother, and Nicky will never be part of my family! Damn you, I loved my mother! You couldn't even get her in the ground before you had Cynthia in front of a justice of the peace!''

''That's a lie and you know it,'' Eugene said in a surprisingly calm tone. ''Cynthia did work for me while your mother was alive, but it wasn't until after her death that we fell in love. Nicky was a delightful surprise, not an accident, and I won't apologize for him. My God, boy, he isn't taking anything away from you! He doesn't even inherit anything except a share of my total estate. Cynthia and I agreed on that from the start! She's got money of her own to settle on him, in case you've forgotten.''

''I've forgotten nothing,'' Cabe told his father in a tone like shattering ice.

Eugene started to speak and then just shrugged, stuffing his hands into his pockets. ''It wouldn't kill you to spend one night with us, all the same. It hurts Nicky that you ignore him.''

''I owe him nothing!''

The older man grimaced and turned away.

Cabe slammed his fist down on Danetta's desk, startling her. She'd put away her coat and was just sitting down to work. ''All right,'' he said angrily. ''Damn it, I'll come for the night.''

''That's my boy,'' Eugene said with an infrequent tenderness. He looked past Cabe at Danetta, who was trying to be invisible. ''Why don't you leave the brassy blonde at home and bring that one with you?'' he mused. ''She keeps an iguana. Nicky would love her.''

Danetta actually gasped. ''How did you know about Norman?'' she asked.

Eugene grinned. "Ask Jenny." His eyes went back to Cabe. "Your secretary here looked pretty flustered when she walked in. I thought maybe you'd—"

"We just came from Harry Deal's oil field," Cabe said with uncommon venom. "She and Harry got into it."

"I hope she won. He's hell on the nerves," Eugene said with a disappointed sigh. "Well, I'll see you tomorrow night," he muttered. "Brassy blonde, God knows how many men—"

"Get out!" Cabe said shortly.

Eugene knew when to quit. He waved at Danetta and walked out without another word.

Danetta was fumbling with the computer, trying to turn it on. Considering how well she did it normally, it was rather disturbing to look like a rank amateur. It had been an upsetting morning.

She smelled cigarette smoke. Cabe came closer with a cigarette in his fingers and stood over her, his pale eyes watchful, his dark, wavy hair falling rakishly onto his broad forehead. He had one hand in his pocket and his chiseled lips were pursed as he looked at her openly and with pure male appreciation.

"I don't have a crush on you," she said, trying to appear calm.

He lifted the cigarette to his mouth and took a long draw from it. "I'm thirteen years older than you," he said quietly. "From a practical standpoint, you don't even have a yardstick to measure me against. Your life is a blank slate." He blew out wispy smoke. "No, I'm the last complication you need in your life, kid," he said shortly. "So no more close encounters. Let's get to work."

He went back into his office with that quick, measured stride that meant he was in a temper. She should have been relieved. But she wasn't. It was like the end of something that hadn't even begun.

She loaded the computer, her heart around her ankles. If he didn't want complications, why did he touch her that way in the car, saying those things to her? Her brows drew into an angry frown. He couldn't resist a little mockery, she supposed. But she wouldn't let him get away with it twice. From now on, she was immune. Or at least, he was going to think she was.

She wondered vaguely who Nicky was. It sounded as if he was a relative, and why would he like Danetta just because she had an iguana? She sighed. Her whole life seemed to be one big question these days.

She started the word processing program and began to type out the routine letters that Cabe had scribbled answers on before they left the office.

Three

___

Danetta sighed over her boss's new and distant attitude in the days that followed. He didn't offer any more conversation that wasn't absolutely necessary, he didn't talk to her unless it was about the job. He didn't even treat her like a younger brother anymore. She had become a piece of office equipment, and he barely looked at her. She'd gone back to her sedate way of dressing, but it probably wouldn't have mattered if she'd come to work nude. He'd said they weren't going to complicate their relationship, and boy, was he keeping his word!

She felt alone, even more than she had when she moved here to stay with her cousin Jenny over two years ago. She'd wanted to be independent, to live her own life, and her parents had supported that need. But now she missed the family. She missed Jenny, because her cousin was a good listener. Jenny was still off in the southwest on some hush-hush assignment. She wished she'd thought to ask Eugene last week if he'd heard from Jenny, but it hadn't been a good time.

She needed someone to talk to because she hadn't realized until now how big a part of her life she'd allowed Cabe Ritter to become. She looked forward to coming to work because he was somehow bigger than life to her. His smile made her tingle, his vibrant masculinity challenged and excited her, his dry wit made her laugh. Just being around him made her feel more alive than she'd ever been before.

She'd had erotic dreams about him ever since that morning in his big Lincoln when he'd woken all her senses with his ardor. But that morning might never have been, because his new attitude was so determinedly business. And Karol was very much in evidence now. Cabe almost seemed to flaunt her, as if he wanted to make sure Danetta didn't get any romantic ideas about him.

She finished the letters she'd been typing and put them aside, her slender fingers lightly resting on the stack. Perhaps he was even trying to freeze her out of his office. The thought made her uneasy. She'd gotten used to his moods and his tempers, and she didn't like the idea of working for anyone else. But if that was what he wanted...

He came in even as she was formulating distasteful plans for her future, and she jumped at the opening of the door.

"Nerves?" he commented. "That's new. What's wrong?"

She handed him the letters with a hand that shook.

"For God's sake!" he burst out. He put down his attaché case, laid the letters aside, and pulled her out of the chair, still holding her hand. "Let's have it. What's wrong?"

"Do you want me to quit?" she asked, her voice uneven.

Every trace of expression left his face. "Do you want to?" He threw the ball back into her court.

She lowered her eyes to his nice white shirt. "It's a good job," she said stiffly. "But if you'd rather I left, I will."

"I don't know what I'd rather," he said heavily. He'd tried not to be aware of her, he'd tried being cold, but it was backfiring. He'd hurt her again, and he felt terrible at her vulnerability. Why couldn't he forget that look on her face when he'd started to kiss her? Why couldn't he find any solace in Karol's company?

With a long sigh, he brought her slender hand against his chest. Under the thin fabric of his shirt, Danetta could feel his chest, the warmth of his body. Cabe was silent as he pressed her fingers against him and he fought the need to do much, much more than that.

She felt herself melting inside. His broad chest felt hard and warm under her hand, yet it felt soft there, too, as if he had hair on his chest. She'd never seen him stripped to the waist, but suddenly she wanted to. She wondered what he looked like under his clothes, and how it would feel if he put his arms around her and kissed her the way he kissed his women, the way he'd whispered to her that he would that morning at Harry Deal's rig.

She drew in a slow, shaky breath. She couldn't seem to breathe properly anymore, and now she knew her mind was going, too. Only a crazy woman would allow herself to be curious in that way about Cabe.

His fingers stroked her neat nails, smoothing over their silky tops. He heard her breathing change and marveled at the way she stood against him, so docile and quiet. It had flattered his ego when Ben Meadows and his father had suggested that shy young Danetta had a crush on him, then it had floored him when he'd made that involuntary pass at her in the car. He hadn't counted on her effect on him, any more than he'd expected her contempt for his life-style—or rather what she thought was his life-style. He'd often wondered what Danetta would do if he made a real pass at her.

He'd been tempted a lot in the past few weeks, thanks to his father's constant remarks about Danetta, bringing her vividly to his attention. She was pretty and she'd begun to disturb him physically. He'd tried ignoring her, but that only made it worse. Now he was touching her, and he knew even as he did it that it was his most regrettable mistake to date.

"Your fingers are like ice," he commented, his voice deep and husky because she smelled of lavender and her softness made such a contrast to the women he'd filled his life with in recent years. Women chased him, but their very aggressiveness irritated him. There was nothing aggressive about Danetta, and she was innocent. Her innocence made his head spin with exquisite fantasies about teaching her the mystery of intimacy. He couldn't forget the look in her eyes when he'd whispered how he wanted to kiss her. . . .

"It's a little chilly in the office," she said. Was that really her own voice, sounding so breathless? "I'll turn the thermostat up."

"Yes, you do that." But he didn't let go of her hand. He pressed it closer and moved it a little, and she could actually feel his heartbeat.

His hand moved to her throat and his thumb pushed under her chin, raising her mouth. He looked down at the soft pink bow of it, at the soft silkiness. His fingers stroked her cheek and his thumb moved lazily to her mouth. He brushed his thumb over it, first gently, then with a rough, abrasive motion that was like a delicate kick in the heart. It was exactly what he'd done before, and it provoked the same shocked delight in her eyes as she looked up at him and a tiny sound worked its way out of her throat.

He liked that sound. He liked even more the shocked sensuality in her eyes as he played with her mouth. She was becoming aroused, much more than she had before. The fascination in her gray eyes spoke for itself. His thumb grew more insistent and her lips parted on a shaky breath. His free hand went to her nape and cradled it firmly, holding her head where he wanted it as he watched her intently.

"This is where the playing stops," he said roughly. "Once my mouth covers yours, there's no going back."

Her gasp was audible. It almost broke the spell. But his eyes were relentless, like that maddening thumb against her mouth, like the helpless trembling of her legs. "It's not fair," she moaned. "Like going fishing with a stick of dynamite..."

"Yes," he agreed softly as he began to lower his head. His eyes shifted to her trembling mouth. "That's how it's going to feel, too. Like dynamite going up. I like it rough," he breathed as his lips parted a breath above hers. "I like it hard and rough. Like this...."

She felt his hand contract at her nape and tasted his warm, smoky breath mingling with hers as she stood there, helpless, all too willing to give him what he wanted.

But even as his lips dragged roughly against hers in a whisper of sensual promise, in the briefest hint of contact, the harsh jingle of the telephone exploded into the tense silence and broke them apart.

Danetta was shaking as if she'd been thrown to the ground. She stared up helplessly at Cabe, oblivious to the source of the loud, irritating noise. He stared back at her, only a little less rattled than she was. Still watching her, he jerked up the receiver and answered it.

"Ritter."

"Cabe, can you take an extra hour off this afternoon to attend a charity dinner with me?" Karol asked him in her soft, cultured voice. "It's to benefit the new children's hospital."

"This afternoon?" he repeated absently. "I suppose so. I'll pick you up at five."

"Lovely! Thank you, darling. See you later."

She hung up but Cabe didn't put down the phone. He was still watching Danetta's shocked eyes.

The silence between them was every bit as explosive now as it had been three minutes ago, but before either of them could speak, Ben Meadows came in the door with a file folder in one hand.

"Sorry to bother you, but I need some copies made," he whispered to Danetta, obviously thinking Cabe was on the telephone.

"I'll...I'll do them." Danetta took the folder with shaking fingers and rushed away to the room where the Xerox machine was kept. Cabe hung up the phone belatedly and took Ben into his office. Danetta did the copies and went back to work as quickly and efficiently as she could.

For the rest of the day, she held her breath, but Cabe didn't come near her again. She wasn't sure if she was glad or sorry, but their relationship had changed forever in those few minutes.

She went home to her lonely apartment, wishing her cousin were home. But the older woman, a ravishing blonde, wasn't due back for a while. Jenny spent most of her working life on expeditions to rustic places, and Danetta knew that it occasionally became dangerous. A man had followed Jenny home once and tried to trail her. Later they'd learned that he was actually an enemy agent, of all things, trying to get information on the geology report Jenny had submitted to Eugene Ritter's company. Those strategic metals she prospected for were important to a lot of people, and not all of the interested parties were Americans.

Even now, Jenny's letters home were full of intriguing innuendos about her job, and Danetta worried about her. She had once secretly envied Jenny that exciting, gypsy existence, but the longer she was around Cabe, the less the life-style appealed. Just lately, the thought of leaving her job was disturbing. She refused to consider why.

She opened the door and there was Jenny, tanned and blond and exuberant.

"Dina!" she exclaimed, hugging the younger woman as she used the childhood nickname she'd always given Danetta. "Oh, how good to be home again!"

"You're not supposed to be here!" Danetta cried, her face showing her surprised pleasure. "But, oh, I'm so glad you are! You look great!"

And she did, too. Her long blond hair fell in soft waves, and her white pantsuit gave her an ultrasophisticated look. Her dark blue eyes sparkled with life as she laughed. Danetta watched her and thought, if only I looked like that. She actually sighed as she put down her purse and kicked off her shoes.

"How long can you stay?" Danetta asked as she went into the kitchen to cook something for supper.

"Overnight," Jenny said, laughing at Danetta's expression. "I'm sorry, love, but I'm en route to a new site. And that's all I can tell you, so don't pry. Nothing to worry about. Except the lounge lizard there." She grimaced, glancing toward the radiator where Norman had draped himself, looking like a small green dinosaur. "Norman keeps staring at me like he wonders how I'd taste."

"He's not a meat eater. He's a vegetarian," Danetta reminded her. She explained the same point every time Jenny came home, and had for the past two years, ever since she'd talked Jenny into letting her bring the small pet into the apartment. Things had been fine until Norman began to grow. But he was undemanding company, house-trained and a walking deterrent to criminals. There had been one attempted break-in, and the perpetrator had run screaming from the apartment, almost colliding with Danetta in his terror. Norman had stood in the doorway with his mouth open, presenting his whip of a tail to lash at the intruder. When he was a few years older, that tail would be a rather dangerous weapon, too. But at the time, Danetta had never been more proud of him. Despite his prowess as a watch-lizard, he was something of a trial to poor Jenny, and he'd frightened away one of her prospective boyfriends who had a terror of saurians.

"What happens if he takes a bite out of me and likes it? Remember Captain Hook and the crocodile?" Jenny mumbled.

"Norman's never had a taste of you." Danetta grinned. "Anyway, he likes you!"

"Does he?" Jenny frowned. "How can you tell?" she mused, watching the lizard's habitually blank expression.

"I can read his mind." Danetta studied her cousin. "I know you love your job, but is it really necessary, all this cloak-and-dagger stuff?"

Jenny laughed delightedly. "Indeed it is. I think of this as a patriotic service to my country. Maybe even to the world, who knows? Now enough about me. Tell me all about you."

"There's nothing to tell," Danetta said with a grin. "I'm not beautiful like you."

"I'm not, you know. I just make the most of what I've got. In fact—" she studied her younger cousin "—so could you. You'd be an absolute dish if you tried. What is this compulsion you have to emulate potted plants and curtains?"

Danetta glared at her. "I am not imitating inanimate objects. I'm just into self-preservation, that's all."

"Knowing your dishy Mr. Ritter, I can understand that," Jenny said with a dry glance. "He'd turn on a brick. But he isn't the only man on earth, Dina. And you're nearing twenty-four already. Don't bury yourself in that office and spend your life eating your heart out for your handsome boss," she added gently.

Danetta's lips parted suddenly. "I'm not eating my heart out for Cabe Ritter!"

"Aren't you?" Jenny got out mayonnaise and bread and put them on the table, pausing to set it with silverware and plates and napkins before she sat down to watch Danetta wielding a knife at the counter. Her blue eyes were soft and concerned. "He's all you ever talk about when I'm home. You haven't dated anyone for over a year, remember."

"I don't want to have to fight off men," Danetta faltered.

"That isn't it. You're besotted with Mr. Ritter."

"That's ridiculous!" she laughed nervously. "Here, have some ham."

Jenny's eyebrows rose as Danetta picked up a plate of cake she'd already sliced and absently offered it to her cousin.

"Uh, Dina, that isn't ham," she said.

The younger woman frowned, glancing from the ham she was slicing to the cake she'd handed her cousin. She could feel her face flaming.

"It's my dull life making me crazy," Danetta sighed. She took back the cake and offered the sliced ham. "Maybe I do need to kiss Norman and see if he turns into a prince."

"That's frogs, not iguanas," Jenny corrected. "But you could use a prince," her cousin added. "A nice tall one who'll treat you like royalty. You'd look right at home in a cottage with a white picket fence and pretty little girls playing around your skirts."

"We both used to dream about that, remember?" Danetta recalled with a smile as she paused long enough to heat up some spinach quiche for Norman and put it in his dog dish. She wondered if anybody made bowls for iguanas. She glanced at Jenny, noticing the withdrawn, sad look on the older woman's face. "Jenny, what's wrong?"

"Nothing," Jenny said quietly. "I'm just tired." She caught the other woman's curious look and smiled. "Nothing's wrong, really. How are Uncle Rob and Aunt Helen?"

Danetta allowed herself to be sidetracked, reluctantly. "Mom and Dad are fine," she said. "They're organizing a youth program back in Missouri that caters to teens on the edge of drug addiction, and they said that your mom is taking up break dancing."

Jenny laughed. "So she wrote me. I hope she doesn't break anything doing it. It's so nice to be home, Dina," she sighed. "Even if it's only for a night."

And it was barely a whole night; when Danetta woke, Jenny was already gone. The twin bed where Jenny had slept was neatly made, and there was a note on it, a very brief one, saying that Jenny had to catch an early flight and would write.

Danetta fed Norman some bananas and avocado and leftover spinach quiche and went to work worrying. Something was going on, and judging by Jenny's look and distracted presence, it was something big.

Jenny had worked on that hush-hush project for the past few months. Her mother, who was Danetta's Aunt Doris, and Danetta's own parents had been uneasy about her taking the job. But Jenny wasn't a homebody, and she seemed to thrive on the excitement.

The thing was, nobody knew or understood what Jenny did. And maybe it was better that way.

Danetta had an office full of people as the day began, which gave her the advantage of not having to spend any time alone with the disturbing Mr. Ritter. After yesterday, she had every intention of walking wide around him. She could have choked herself senseless for letting him get that close, for letting him see how vulnerable she was.

But he was, again, all business, even if she did feel the heat of his gaze more often than usual as the day wore on.

Lunchtime came, and Danetta got her purse to run down to the small Chinese restaurant at the corner and get the takeout she'd ordered. She usually ate at her desk except when one of the women from the other offices in the building invited her to join them, and that wasn't too often these days. It seemed that everyone was suffering from work pressure.

"Can I bring you anything from the Chinese place?" Danetta asked Cabe politely, pausing in the open doorway of his office.

"No, thanks," he said with forced indifference. He was still having hell trying to keep his distance from her after yesterday. "I'm taking Karol to lunch." She nodded and started to leave, stopped by his curt, "Dan?"

She turned, grateful to hear even that hated nickname if it meant he was mellowing a little. "Yes, sir?"

His blue eyes narrowed and with helpless fascination he studied her slender figure in the gray crepe dress. "You've been very quiet today."

"I've been busy," she said. "And I didn't get much sleep last night."

He scowled. "Why not?"

He had no right to ask, but the answer popped out automatically. "I had company. Well, until just before dawn, anyway," she began, wondering how much she should tell him about Jenny.

The look on his face was almost comical. It seemed to actually pale. He sat up, his expression going from mild surprise to anger in the space of seconds. "I thought one-night-stands weren't your style."

"One-night . . . Oh, I see. No, not a man," she blurted out. "My cousin, Jenny."

He made an odd gesture with one hand, looking as surprised as she felt, because the question shouldn't have been asked or answered. His eyes caught hers and held them, and that long, sweet electricity flowed between them as potently as it had the day before. Her smile faded and she felt her heartbeat racing in her throat as his eyes darkened. She saw the muscles in his firm, stubborn chin clench as he stared back at her with blue lightning flashing in his eyes, as if he were struggling for control.

In fact he was, but before he could move or speak, Karol walked in, wearing a light colored, gauzy dress with a matching ribbon in her long, silky blond hair. Cabe got to his feet with quiet grace, tearing his eyes away from Danetta and forcing a smile for Karol as she joined them.

"Well, well, what a pretty decoration for my office," he murmured, his voice falling an octave as Karol nodded and smiled coolly at Danetta before she walked past her to Cabe.

"You flatterer," Karol said.

"I wouldn't call it flattery," Cabe returned. Danetta was beginning to get under his skin in a big way, and he couldn't have those long, soulful looks coming at him day after day without doing something about her. He had to show Danetta that she meant nothing to him, for her own sake. He could hurt her badly if he let this go any further. He couldn't afford the luxury of getting involved with a naive little virgin who didn't know beans about men or life. And there was one sure way to do that, he thought with sudden insight.

He reached out to Karol, caught her close and bent to kiss her with fierce, rough ardor, right in front of a shocked, embarrassed Danetta.

"I'd better go," Danetta stammered, managing somehow to drag her eyes away from them and creep out the door without anyone noticing.

All the way down the elevator, and to the restaurant, she couldn't get the sight out of her mind. It hurt, and she didn't understand why. Cabe, with that beautiful woman in his arms, his mouth so violently hungry on hers, his arms corded around her, pressing her to every lean inch of his powerful body. Danetta almost groaned out loud at the memory, wondering how it would feel to have him treat her that way. She had to stop this, she told herself firmly. She was letting his charm blind her to what was underneath it. Karol was just a conquest, like all his other conquests, and Danetta's parents hadn't raised her to be just a name in some man's black book.

She deliberately took her time getting back to her office, so that Cabe and Karol were gone when she returned with her lunch. She was sitting behind her desk halfheartedly picking at her Moo Goo Gai Pan when Ben Meadows peered in the door, his blond head gleaming as he grinned at her.

"All alone?" he murmured. "Unprotected?"

"Not really," she replied with a mischievous smile. "I'm armed with deadly kung fu chopsticks. Ha!" She made a mock lunge with one.

"You wouldn't really attack a hardworking sales manager, would you?"

She shook her head. "Want some Moo Goo?" she offered.

He made a horrible face. "I won't eat something with a name like that."

"It's just chicken and oriental vegetables in sauce, and it's delicious."

"That's what they told me about spinach quiche," he said with a glare. "Anyway, how about a nice leisurely

lunch in an expensive restaurant with white wine and fat-
tening desserts? On me,'' he added, smiling hopefully.

She studied him curiously. He wasn't bad looking, and
he was much closer to her age than Cabe. A nice, steady
man who never chased women, who was very quiet as a rule
and never made trouble. She liked him, although she didn't
know him socially. Not for lack of effort on his part; he was
forever asking her out and she was forever refusing. But
since Cabe had said that about her refusing Meadows because she had a crush on her boss, she changed her mind.

''I'd have loved to,'' she said with a smile. ''But I'm almost through now.''

''Tomorrow,'' he said quickly. ''How about tomorrow?''

''I'd love to, Ben,'' she replied. ''Thank you.''

''Great . . . I . . . oh, no,'' he groaned. ''Wait a minute, I
have to be out of town until Wednesday. So how about
Thursday?'' he altered the invitation hopefully.

She smiled. ''That would be fine, Ben,'' she said softly.

He grinned. ''Thursday, then. We'll go somewhere fancy,
so dress for it, okay?''

''Okay!''

He went down the hall whistling, and Danetta finished
her lunch, hoping she hadn't made a bad choice. He'd only
been with the company a month or so, but he seemed very
nice, and it would do her good to go out for once. Sitting
at home was suddenly appalling.

Cabe didn't come back until well after two-thirty, and he
looked disheveled. It didn't take much imagination to figure out what he'd been doing with his lady friend. Danetta
spared him one quick glance and then got on with her work,
giving him pleasant, polite answers when he asked questions, doing her job and trying to camouflage the hurt he'd
inflicted.

Cabe had noticed that wounded look and nodded to himself with grim, guilty satisfaction while he tried to reassure himself that he had a noble excuse for his actions. Karol didn't like to be mussed, so he'd mussed himself to appear as if he and his lady had done more than eat and talk for two hours. It had worked, if Danetta's expression was any indication. Now she'd get the idea and her crush would die a natural death. That was necessary, he told himself. He didn't want to hurt her any more than he already had. If only there hadn't been such pain in those soft gray eyes... He groaned out loud. Hurting her was the last thing he'd wanted to do, but he had nothing to give her. A brief affair was the only thing he had to offer, and that would be cruel in the extreme. Danetta deserved so much more than his raw desire. But she was vulnerable and so was he. He'd have succumbed to those soft, soulful looks eventually, so he had to stop them. Now he had, but it gave him no pleasure. He couldn't even bear to look at her.

He wondered sometimes what she'd think if she knew the truth, knew how alone he really was, how few women there'd actually been in his life. The playboy image was very useful in its way. It kept serious contenders from getting too close to him, from seeing that he was every bit as fastidious in his private life as the ice-cold Karol. Actually Karol was a business acquaintance who'd had a raw deal with men and wanted no intimate complications. She and Cabe dated to protect each other, and it was working very well. Thank God there would be no more temptation from Danetta. He hadn't realized just how badly he'd wanted her. Thank God Ben had interrupted them, or anything might have happened. As it was, he could pretend that it had been a momentary lapse, but he had to make sure it wasn't repeated, ever.

Danetta had gotten the idea, though, and it showed when she left work at quitting time.

She finished at five and despite the fact that she was usually the last one out of the office, she left on time without bothering to say goodbye to Mr. Ritter. She spent an uncomfortable evening in front of the television, the silence broken only by the occasional and rare movements Norman made as he moved from the radiator to his paper in the bathroom and back again.

She fed him and wondered what Cabe would think of him. She already knew that her boss was afraid of nothing in the world except snakes. She frowned. Technically Norman was a reptile, even though he had legs. Would Mr. Ritter be afraid of him? Maybe someday she'd find out.

"I don't suppose iguanas turn into princes, Norman," she sighed, watching him scramble onto the radiator and sprawl as if he were boneless. He glanced at her indifferently and closed his eyes. "Oh, well," she confessed, "even if you were a prince under a spell, I'm not kissing you. Although," she murmured darkly, "I'd rather kiss you than Mr. Ritter. At least I know where you've been."

That set her off, as she remembered his father's comment about Karol. She laughed all the way to bed, trying her best to put the sight of Karol in Cabe's arms out of her mind.

She didn't sleep well that night, and only the thought of a luxury lunch with Ben Meadows kept her going for the next two days. That, she thought, would show Mr. Ritter that she wasn't dying of unrequited love for him.

Cabe himself was quietly polite, except to glance at her from time to time in a brooding way, as if he were worried about something. The rest of the time, his blue eyes smoldered as they slid with pointed appreciation over her soft curves.

She ignored his scrutiny. Probably he was afraid that after he'd kissed Karol so ardently, Danetta's heart was broken and she was going to jump off the roof or something and embarrass him. Well, once she went out with Ben, he'd be reassured and things would get back to normal, she told herself.

Meanwhile she'd dressed to the hilt for Ben's sake, and she looked even better than she had the day she and Cabe had gone out to Mr. Deal's oil rig.

She'd left her curly permed light brown hair long and wavy around her shoulders and down her back. She'd put on more makeup than usual, emphasizing her long lashes, her big gray eyes and her exquisite complexion. She wore a red lipstick that highlighted her mouth, just the shade to match her sexy red-and-white shirtwaist dress. It was a clingy fabric that lovingly outlined her high, full breasts, small waist, flaring hips and long, sexy legs. She wore red high heels that gave her even more height than usual. It had both disturbed and unnerved her that Cabe had hardly been able to take his eyes off her all morning. And when Ben came to pick her up for their date, he just stood in the doorway and sighed, smiling at her dreamily.

That amused her and she laughed, the sound pleasant and musical. Cabe Ritter came out of his office in time to see her face, and something explosive flashed in his blue eyes.

"Do you need something, Ben?" he asked pointedly, because he didn't like the way Ben was looking at her—not one bit.

"No, Cabe. I came to pick up Danetta for our lunch date," the younger man said pleasantly, too intent on her to notice Cabe's shocked expression turn suddenly to anger. "I'll have her back by one sharp, I promise. Danetta, shall we go?"

Cabe stood rigidly watching them leave, his mind whirling with new complications. He'd inadvertently shoved her right into Ben's waiting arms, and he knew things about Ben that she wouldn't. He wanted to stand in the middle of the floor and curse. He'd have to nip that situation in the bud, and quick. But how?

He sighed angrily, jamming his big, lean hands into the pockets of his gray slacks. Life had been so simple and rewarding until he'd started to kiss Danetta at Christmas. His body had given him hell ever since, and Eugene had escalated things with his running commentary on Danetta. Now he was torn between desire and nobility, and Ben was running off with the girl. Ben, who was a shady character at best where women were concerned. He felt guilty because he knew Danetta would never have gone out with Ben if he hadn't pushed her into it. But his motives had been honorable, damn it. He didn't seduce virgins, which Danetta certainly was.

The thing was, Ben wouldn't be as concerned about Danetta's chastity. Like most modern men, his sales manager felt that all women were fair game and to him casual sex was part of his life-style. He'd think nothing of seducing Danetta if he could, and he wouldn't understand her guilt or shame, because that wasn't part of the game.

Cabe's eyes darkened angrily as he saw the whole horrible mess develop in his mind. Well, Ben wasn't leaving Danetta pregnant and alone, not if Cabe had to load his .30-.30 and point him toward a minister. Then he thought about Danetta, living miserably with a man who had no sense of morality, and mentally put the rifle back in the closet. No, that wouldn't do. He'd take care of her himself, and the baby. He pursed his lips, thinking about a pretty little girl in a frilly dress. He could buy her things. Or if it were a boy, he could roughhouse with him in the yard and teach him about the oil business. A little boy would be very nice....

"...I said, do you want me to have Mr. Samples call you back, Mr. Ritter, or do you want to speak with him?" Ben's secretary was asking him politely from the doorway.

The vacant smile fell from his lips and he scowled, wondering how Ben's secretary had gotten into the fantasy he'd been having of the house with his adoptive child. He cleared his throat as he realized he'd been daydreaming.

"Sorry. I'll take the call," he said absently and went back into his office. Just as well that Danetta's little boy was only a fantasy, he thought as he reached for the telephone. He didn't really have time right now to play with kids.

Four

———

Danetta had never been inside such a fancy restaurant except once with Jenny's mother and father years ago. The decor was exquisite, and the menu was liberally sprinkled with French words that Danetta barely remembered from her high-school French class. She chose a chicken dish that wouldn't be too hard on Ben's pocket and watched, amused, while he opted for steak and lobster and a bottle of imported white wine.

"Only one glass for me," Danetta insisted with a smile when they were through with their meal. Ben had refilled his glass and started to pour more into her glass as she covered it with her hand. "I don't have the head for even mild forms of alcohol."

"Oh?" Ben grinned. "I'll have to remember that."

"You devil," she teased. She sipped the dry wine, liking its delicate flavor. "It was nice of you to invite me out."

"I'd like to make a habit of it," he replied, searching her face with purely appreciative eyes. "I thought you'd never say yes."

"I don't date very much," she confessed. "You see, I'm not a liberated girl."

He lifted both eyebrows. "Really?" he teased, obviously taking her remark with a grain of salt.

"Really."

He studied her for a long moment and actually laughed. "If that's true, then you're unique, and I salute you," he said, lifting his glass in a toast. "But you're the first of Cabe's secretaries who could make that claim. Not that he's a bad man. He isn't. He just likes women."

She sighed. "So I've heard," she replied. "But he doesn't like me; not in the way you mean, anyway."

"He's blind," he said, smiling gently. "You're a dish."

She flushed. "Thank you."

He pursed his lips and studied his glass. "Any more like you at home?" he asked with an odd inflection.

"I'm an only child." She grinned. "I've got a beautiful cousin, but she doesn't spend much time at home."

"Why not?" he asked very casually.

She proceeded to tell him why, her tongue loosened by the white wine. But after a few minutes, she became aware that she was babbling. "Sorry. I guess the wine went to my head."

"Everything about you fascinates me, as it happens," he said quickly. "And your cousin sounds like a really interesting lady. Too bad she can't put down roots."

"That's what I think, too."

"I guess you like sharing an apartment with her," he murmured, "since you've got it to yourself most of the time."

"Yes, I really do. She was home earlier in the week, but only overnight." She laughed and put down her glass. "Gosh, Ben, that stuff is potent!"

"So they say." He pursed his lips again, studying her quietly. "I'd like to get to know you, Danetta Marist, if you're on the level, and the corporate wolf doesn't have your name in his book. I don't want to step on Mr. Ritter's toes."

"I don't belong to Mr. Ritter," she informed him. She frowned. "I never realized people thought I did."

"Not people," he said. "Just me." He shrugged. "I'm new in the company. All I know about people is what I hear."

"Where did you work before?" she asked with a smile.

"In California," he said, and abruptly changed the subject. "Tell me about this geology stuff. That's old man Ritter's company that your cousin works for, isn't it? I thought Cabe Ritter had an interest in it when I came to work here, but he doesn't seem to."

"Oh, no, he and his father don't get along." She shook her head. "I guess he'll inherit it one day, but he's strictly in the equipment business right now. I doubt he even knows what Eugene's doing."

Ben said something under his breath and took a sip of wine. For a minute he looked distant, then he studied Danetta again. "Well, I guess your cousin leads an exciting life. Does she ever tell you about her jaunts?"

Something about this sounded odd, but she was too dizzy to consider it.

"Not a word, it's all hush-hush, like James Bond." Danetta chuckled, liking her little joke. "But she draws strange pictures of things." She frowned. "She had this geology map that she traced and marked on. She forgot it, too. I'll have to put it in the mail to her tomorrow."

Ben brightened. "Map, huh? I'd love to see a real geology map."

"Oh, I couldn't show you," she said with an apologetic smile. "She'd be mad. Why did you think I was having an affair with the boss?" she added curiously.

"No reason, really," he murmured absently. "Just the way he looked at you the other day. But there's Karol Sarain, of course," he said, smiling indifferently. "So he may actually be caught this time," he chuckled. "From what I hear, Karol doesn't sleep around. If he's got it bad for her, he'll have to marry her first. That's a lady with a first-class brain," he added absently. "Very thorough. She'll go far in the business world. I've known her for a couple of years. She dated an uncle of mine once."

Danetta didn't want to talk about Karol. In fact she felt sick. She moved her wineglass and saw her hand shake on the stem. It was ridiculous to feel so miserable. She knew that Cabe Ritter was a playboy, and she knew he'd dated nobody except Karol for weeks. Why should she care, anyway? Ben liked her.

"You okay?" Ben asked, frowning.

"Of course. The wine's gone to my head. I'm sorry," she apologized. "I'm not used to it."

"No problem. I'll guide you back to the office." He chuckled. "I'll even carry you up the elevator shaft if you like."

"You're a prince, Ben," she told him warmly.

"I wish the boss paid me like one," he sighed. "Salaries round here are the pits, Danetta. Okay, if you're ready, we'll go."

"I enjoyed lunch," she told him, smiling wanly.

"We'll do it again," he promised, and held her waist firmly as he guided her toward the counter, to keep her from wobbling.

Ben got her to the office and put her inside, smiling at her worried look. "Don't let him upset you," he whispered, hearing Cabe moving around in the next room. "You're over twenty-one. You can drink at lunch if you like."

"Yes, I can," she agreed. "See you later. Thanks again."

He winked and left, closing the door firmly behind him.

The sound brought a worried, irritated Cabe out of his office to meet her, his eyes cold. "You took your sweet time," he said shortly. He'd been pacing for an hour, snapping at people on the phone. And here she was looking as if Ben had drowned her in wine. He had a bad feeling about the whole thing. He hated the possessiveness she aroused in him, the protective instinct. He'd never felt that before.

It had been a long time since she'd seen him bristle that much. He could be intimidating when he liked. He was all muscle, and those blue eyes could burn like ice when he wanted them to. They were doing it now. With his slightly wavy hair disheveled and down on his scowling brow, his dark, hard face drawn with anger, he made Danetta uncomfortable.

"It's only five minutes until one," she mumbled, putting down her purse. The wine made her face hot, and prodded her temper. She glared back at him. "I wonder how many people in the building think I'm sleeping with you?" she blurted out, still irritated by Ben's assumption that she was Cabe's lover.

He couldn't have looked more surprised if someone had hit him in the back of the head with a tire iron. "I beg your pardon?" he asked.

"Ben thought you were sleeping with me. He said you had a great track record with your secretaries."

He glanced toward the door with blazing eyes. "Damn Ben," he said shortly. "I'll break his neck."

Danetta was afraid he meant immediately, so she got in front of him, regretting her impulsive outburst. Now he'd kill Ben and she'd go to jail as an accessory to murder.

"You can't," she said. Her voice sounded funny. Slurred. She cleared her throat. "You can't go around killing people during the lunch hour, there's nobody to clean up the mess."

The anger seemed to leave him. He stopped just in front of her, so close that the clean fragrance of his body filled her nostrils seductively. He looked down at her quietly, his eyes reluctantly appraising her, registering her soft, blatant femininity that stirred his body to anguished life.

"I don't sleep with my secretaries," he said. "As you yourself ought to know after two years." He leaned closer, his eyebrows rising. "You reek of white wine. How much did you have?"

"I don't reek," she said indignantly. "I only had one little big glass of the stuff." That sounded funny and she giggled. "Sorry." She wiped off the smile. "One big little glass, I meant."

"You don't drink, you young idiot," he muttered. "You'd better go home."

"I'm not drunk! Look, I can even walk a straight...oops, sorry," she muttered when she bumped into him.

He swung her up into his arms and she sighed, clinging to his neck as he turned and carried her back into his office, kicking the door shut behind him.

He was as strong as she'd imagined, her weight seemingly inconsequential to him. She stared up at his hard face with helpless fascination, because only once had she been this close to him. She would start remembering the way he'd kissed Karol, she thought miserably as her gaze fell to the chiseled perfection of his sensuous mouth. She loved being carried by him, and she wanted him to bend and kiss her the way he'd threatened to once, hard and rough, and with his mouth open....

He felt that stare and wanted to groan out loud. She was half lit. He couldn't take advantage of it, despite the fact that her dress outlined every soft curve of her exquisite body and fired his blood so suddenly that his own arousal startled him.

"What are you going to do with me?" she asked in a husky whisper.

His darkened blue eyes met hers as he stopped at the long leather couch. "Don't put any ideas in my head," he said stiffly. His chest rose and fell heavily. "I had in mind stretching you out here until the effects of your lunch wear off. I'll make some coffee."

"I can't lie down in your office," she protested as he leaned over to put her down gently, letting her head rest on the padded arm of the sofa.

"Why can't you?" he asked.

Damn the sofa arm, he thought angrily, because it tilted her head at just the right angle to make her soft bow of a mouth look enticing. He poised above her trying to think, trying to make his body listen to his brain while her soft arm remained curled around his neck.

"Do you sleep with Karol?" she whispered.

He did groan. His hand slid into her hair and grasped a soft handful. "You can't ask me questions like that," he ground out.

"Why not? You say all sorts of outrageous things to me!"

His eyes slid over her relaxed body, lingering helplessly on the soft, sweet curves that the dress did not disguise. He wanted to ravish her where she lay. He wanted to take off her clothes and have her, right there, and glory in the pleasure her body would give him. He clenched his teeth. "No, I don't sleep with Karol," he said harshly. His hand bit into her waist, holding her still. "You need coffee," he said firmly, emphasizing every single syllable because that kept him from thinking how it would feel to strip her naked and bury himself in her. He had to remember that she was a virgin. "I'm going to make a pot of coffee, right now."

"Why?" she asked, her body moving helplessly on the leather as she looked up at him, her soft gray eyes so sensuous that he went taut all over again.

"Because, God help me, if I don't, I'll have you where you lay," he muttered to himself with feverish need in his strained voice. "Now stay put!"

He dragged himself to his feet and turned away from her, moving toward the small kitchen area in one corner of his elegant office. His body was throbbing painfully, but he forced his feet to move. Coffee would solve all his problems right now. Certainly it would. Everything would be fine if he could just keep himself from looking over his shoulder where Danetta was sprawled like a virgin sacrifice.

She sighed, stretching, her eyes on the powerfully built man fumbling with the coffeepot. Funny, she couldn't remember ever seeing him fumble, and he'd said something incredible about her if she could only remember what. She felt really good. Light-headed. Delightfully boneless. Nothing mattered anymore. She hummed to herself, raising one leg lazily, idly noticing the fabric sliding down to her hips, leaving her long, elegant legs in their silky hose bare and pretty. She didn't have bad legs, she thought, even if she couldn't win a beauty contest.

Cabe had started the coffee, and turned back just as the skirt of her dress slid away. His jaw clenched. God, he'd never seen anything half that lovely, and the way she looked today, he couldn't blame Ben for taking her out. The miracle was that he'd been able to bring her back. She really was something when she dressed properly and emphasized her assets. And what assets they were, he thought, studying her boldly.

She turned her head a little, aware of his blatant stare. He'd never looked at her like *that* before, she told herself. But even with alcohol fogging her mind, she knew that she shouldn't encourage him. He was a playboy, and she certainly wasn't cut out to be a one-night stand.

With a faint sigh, she turned over on her side, pulling her skirt discreetly down as she closed her eyes sleepily.

Cabe watched her with turbulent emotion. Why had Ben encouraged her to drink like that? His new sales manager had been exhibiting some odd behavior lately, and he was sporting a new Jaguar. Cabe knew his financial situation, and he was certain that the younger man couldn't afford a set of wheels like that on what he was being paid at Ritter Equipment Corporation. He frowned, brooding over Danetta's sensuous figure while he answered two phone calls and checked the outer office for customers. Fortunately it was a slow day.

He poured a cup of very strong black coffee and sat down beside her, touching her shoulder lightly to awaken her.

She opened her eyes and stared up at him blankly. Then she smiled, and it was like sunshine on a rainy morning. "Hi," she murmured.

"Hi, yourself," he replied tersely. "God, what a headache you're going to have. Here. Sit up and drink this."

She dragged herself up, facing him, her body still feeling boneless. He had to help her hold the cup while she took several brief sips.

"It's too strong," she complained.

"It has to be," he replied. "I can't run the office by myself."

She caught her breath. It suddenly dawned on her where she was, who she was, and what she did for a living. "Oh,

I'm so sorry, Mr. Ritter," she blurted out. She colored violently. "Ben bought this expensive bottle of white wine, and I didn't really want any, but it seemed impolite to say no when he'd paid so much for it."

He scowled. None of this made much sense, least of all Ben's sudden interest in Danetta. Ben was the real playboy in the company, although he was relatively discreet. He liked the hard-drinking, hard-playing kind of woman, and Danetta certainly wasn't that.

"Your parents should have encouraged you to date a few rakes while you were in your teens," he said unexpectedly, still scowling as he studied her flushed face. "You don't have the experience to recognize one."

She lifted her eyebrows. "Certainly I do," she said. "I work for one."

He searched her soft, gray eyes but didn't smile. "The image is convenient," he said. "I encourage it. But don't make the mistake of thinking that I'm everything I seem to be."

That didn't make sense. Of course, nothing else did, either. She sipped more of the coffee. "Ben's nice."

He glared at her. "I gather he's the reason for the change from your regular uniform?" he asked, his blue eyes sliding down her body.

"I don't wear a uniform," she protested.

"Long skirts and granny blouses and your hair in a bun," he said curtly. "You never come to the office looking like you do today. Except once," he bit off, remembering too vividly the occasion.

"I am aware that sexy women are endangered when in the company of rakes," she said with deliberate enunciation. "You said not to give you the wrong idea."

"I said a lot of things," he replied angrily.

"You were right about that," she said, wondering why he was so angry. "I don't do one-night stands, and you wouldn't want a secretary that you'd ... seduced. I only dressed up for Ben today."

He took a slow breath, his eyes holding hers. "Danetta, as difficult as it may be to convince you of this, I don't do one-night stands, either," he said quietly. "In fact, I don't sleep around. I never have."

She stifled a giggle. "Sure."

He raised an eyebrow. "Only a child like you would accept a facade like mine."

"The way you kissed Karol the other day was no facade," she shot back, outraged all over again at being an involuntary witness to that ardent assault.

He watched her sudden color with interest. "I didn't say I was totally inexperienced. I just said that I don't sleep around."

"Then why let everyone think you do?"

His sensuous mouth curved up at one corner. "Because it keeps marriage-minded women out of my hair. No sane homebody goes after a playboy with happily ever after in mind."

"No, I guess not." She wasn't sure if she was really hearing this or if she was still in an alcoholic stupor. She pinched herself and grimaced, just to make sure.

"You aren't dreaming. Your head will tell you that later," he mused. He brushed the untidy hair away from her face, his fingers slow and tender. "Did it bother you, watching me kiss Karol?" he asked unexpectedly, and saw the answer in her expression.

She finished her coffee with hands that tremored faintly. "I'm better now," she said. "I'll get back to work."

But he didn't move, and she couldn't. His hand brushed her cheek, resting there while his thumb smoothed lazily over her soft lips.

His blue eyes began to darken, to narrow. "Has a man ever twisted you into his body that way and put his mouth against yours as if he'd die to have it?"

She turned scarlet. "Men don't feel that way about women like me," she said, averting her gaze to his jacket. It was a silky light gray, very becoming. The white shirt and red patterned tie under it emphasized the darkness of his skin, and he smelled of expensive cologne. He was too close again.

"Why don't they?" he asked. His fingers trailed lightly down her throat, making her weak.

"I'm not...not the kind of woman who inspires violent emotions," she stammered. "I'm old-fashioned and quiet and..."

"And exquisitely sexy," he breathed as his warm mouth brushed softly against hers in a shocking, sweet contact. He lifted his head and searched her face, assessing her helpless response with pure pleasure. "Give me that," he said softly. He took the coffee cup, empty now, and put it on the coffee table before he turned back to her. His eyes were darker now, smoldering with emotion, and there wasn't a trace of expression on his hard features. He framed her face in his lean, warm hands and drew her mouth up under his.

"You said...the other day..." she faltered, trying to think when all she knew was the warm whisper of his breath on her lips.

"I said that once my mouth covered yours, there was no going back," he whispered. His hands tightened. "I meant it. Don't pull away from me. Let me fit my mouth to yours...let me open yours, the way I told you I would...Danetta!"

He did that, slowly, with deadly mastery, so that she lost the will to resist almost immediately. Her eyes closed helplessly as the hard, warm crush of his mouth began to burn on hers, his lips pushing hers apart, the kiss growing steadily more intimate until her breath mingled with his and she could feel his tongue stealing inside her mouth.

She stiffened and gasped, startled by the invasion. That kind of kiss was one she'd always avoided with her infrequent dates, but Cabe wouldn't let her pull back. One big hand slid to her nape and trapped her mouth against his while his tongue shot inside it, in slow, deep thrusts that made her body clench.

She moaned. Her nails bit into his broad shoulders, into the fabric of his jacket, and she shuddered as the rhythm of his penetrating tongue became violent, as he groaned harshly against her mouth and she felt his hands tremble where they held her face.

The danger of what was happening filtered through to his brain, even as his body was beginning to tense in agony. He had to force himself to lift his head, and when he saw Danetta's sensuous, rapt face, it took all his willpower not to take her mouth a second time.

Her eyes opened, soft like a gray mist, trusting, faintly hungry and a little dazed. Her mouth was swollen and trembling.

He searched her eyes in a heady silence, his hands smoothing her hair while he fought for control of himself. "French kisses weren't allowed before this, I gather?" he asked huskily.

"You...made me," she managed, her voice thready and high-pitched as she came down from the heights he'd taken her to.

"Yes." He touched her sensitized lips, masculine appreciation in his narrow eyes. "You need teaching," he said huskily. "You even taste virginal."

Her heartbeat shook her as she met his gaze. It had never been like that with anyone. The intimacy still unnerved her, because it had been so suggestive. Would it be that way in bed, she wondered helplessly; would he insist if she resisted the stark intimacy, would he make her give in to him....

"It was only a kiss, Danetta," he said, his voice deep and quiet. "Nothing to be afraid of."

"It would be like that...in bed," she whispered, so shattered that she voiced her thoughts.

His expression hardened, his eyes began to burn. "Yes," he ground out. "Exactly like that. You'd pull back out of fear and I'd hold you to me, I'd gentle you in the sweetest kind of way, and you'd yield to my body. And then you'd stop being afraid and it would be like fires burning in the darkness, like thunder in a black sky. You'd resist, but only for a few seconds. Then you'd want me back, and you and I would go up in flames."

Her body trembled at the pictures in her mind, and she knew that he was doing it deliberately. His eyes held hers, unblinking, watching her reactions.

"One day," he said huskily, "I'll have you. In spite of everything, you'll lie in my arms and give yourself to me."

She couldn't breathe. He pulled her face into his throat and wrapped her up in a rough, tight embrace, his powerful arms contracting until she was crushed to him, drowning in the scent and feel of him. She should have protested that last statement, she should have said something. But she already knew that it was the truth. If she didn't get away from this office, it was going to happen. Now that she'd had a taste of him, it wouldn't be enough. She closed her eyes and wanted to cry. She'd been afraid of this moment subconsciously since the very first day she'd walked into the office, since her first sight of the elegant and very sexy Mr. Ritter with his icy pale eyes and sensuous mouth.

She felt him move, felt her body descend to the sofa. He was easing her down, and the look on his face was exciting and terrifying, because he looked like a man whose control had snapped. His eyes were burning into hers, his hands held a faint tremor as they lifted her backward onto the couch. She watched him, helpless, her body as hungry as her eyes, confused by her own reactions to his potent ardor.

"Hello?"

They both jumped at the loud voice coming from the waiting room. He let go of Danetta and stood erect, scowling down at her while he tried to make his mind work.

"Is anybody here?" the loud, half angry voice came again.

"My God," Cabe breathed, his eyes holding Danetta's for just a second before he straightened, turned on his heel and went out into the waiting room.

He'd closed the door behind him. Danetta threw her shaky legs over the edge of the sofa and struggled to her feet. She was still unsteady, but the coffee was beginning to work. She took her cup to the pot and poured it full again, leaning back against his bookcase to sip it. Her life had become too complicated for words in the past few days. She stared into the coffee dazedly. Was she delirious, or had Cabe Ritter just kissed her into blind submission?

She finished the coffee just as he came back into the office, somber and a little distant.

"Feeling better?" he asked.

She nodded. "I'm very sorry," she repeated numbly. "I didn't mean to get sauced at lunch, and I won't do it again. I..." She glanced at the sofa and blushed, avoiding his eyes. "I'll just get back to work, now."

She put down the cup and started toward the door. He looked as if he might reach out and catch her on the way, but he leaned back against his desk instead, his hands on the edges, the knuckles turning white.

Her hand paused on the doorknob of the outer office. "I apologize for the way I acted just now," she said expressively, still with her back to him. "It was the wine. I've never done anything like that before. I hope it didn't give you the wrong idea," she faltered.

"No," he said softly. "There's nothing to be embarrassed about, Danetta."

She gritted her teeth. "And I am sorry, Mr. Ritter."

"My name is Cabe," he said, his voice quiet, very deep.

"Yes, I know, but..."

"If you'd rather not use it when we've got clients in the office, I don't mind. But when we're alone, I don't want to be called Mr. Ritter again."

She mustered enough courage to glance at him, fascinated by the expression on his face. Tenderness mingled with soft indulgence lay there, and his blue eyes were without their usual hardness.

"All right, Cabe," she said in a barely audible whisper.

His eyes slid down to her mouth and lingered there possessively. He thought about the deep, intimate kiss they'd shared and his body tautened at the pleasure it brought back. She was exciting to make love to. Dangerously exciting. She was a virgin and she'd expect to marry the first man who stormed the citadel of her innocence. Why couldn't he make himself remember that?

"Get me Howard Drake on the phone, will you?" he asked suddenly, and forced himself to move behind the desk and sit down.

"Yes, sir," she replied. She went back to her own desk and placed the call for him. It was going to be a challenge to put this day behind her. It was like a turning point in her life, but where it would lead, she couldn't guess.

Five

Between her headache and what had happened earlier, Danetta was more than ready to leave at five. Cabe watched her get her things together with a brooding stare, leaning against the doorway of his office with his hands in his pockets.

"Will you be all right?" he asked.

She smiled at his concern. "Yes, thank you. I'll know not to drink wine like water the next time."

His face tautened. "Is there going to be a next time? Ben's a nice boy, but he's too slick for an innocent like you."

She gasped. "Look who's talking!" she blurted out.

He stared her down. "I won't take advantage. He would. That's the difference."

She wondered what he considered taking advantage, but she was too embarrassed and flustered to ask. She got into her coat and held her purse against her breast like a shield.

"Well . . . good night."

He sighed heavily. "Good night, honey. I won't fuss if you're late in the morning."

Surely she hadn't heard that endearment. She glanced back at him, puzzled and touched by his changed attitude even as she tried not to let herself read too much into it.

"Good night, Mr.—" his glare cut her off "—I mean . . . Cabe."

The way she said his name disturbed him. He searched her soft eyes for a long moment and electricity seemed to crackle between them.

"Oh, there you are, Danetta," Ben Meadows called from the open door. "Come on, I'll walk you down to the bus stop!"

"Thanks, Ben. Good night," she said again, turning away from the black glare she was getting from Cabe as she went out the door with Ben.

Cabe stared after them with mixed emotions. She was vulnerable and Ben was a ladies' man. For two cents, he'd follow along, just to make sure Ben didn't make a heavy pass while she was too dizzy to say no. But he didn't have the right, he reminded himself. And if he interfered, Danetta might wonder why; she might realize that he was vulnerable, too.

He turned back into his office and slammed the door—hard. Well, he had plenty of work to do. There was no need for him to rush home, if his spartan apartment could be called that. He sat down at his desk and opened the drawer, pulling out the latest sales figures.

Danetta rode the bus to her apartment building in a daze. It had been that kind of day. Her head was full of dreams as she went up in the elevator and walked toward her apartment when she reached her floor. She inserted her key in the lock, humming softly to herself—and noticed that the door opened before the key was turned.

Instantly alert, she pushed the door all the way open and caught her breath at what she saw. Every drawer had been emptied, her books had been dumped out of the book-cases, the sofa cushions were out of their covers. All her pots and pans were dumped on the counter, all her mail opened and scattered.

She leaned against the wall for support. Her first thought was of Norman, and if whoever had done this to her apartment had hurt him.

"Norman!" she called. She picked up the iron that she kept in her closet and, brandishing it like a weapon, left the door open and crept hesitantly into the living room, look-ing everywhere. More than likely her messy visitor was long gone, but she couldn't afford to assume that.

She opened the bedroom door, finding the same disar-ray in there that the combination living-dining-kitchen area had shown. But the bedroom was empty, like the closet and bathroom. With a heavy sigh, she closed the door and put the chain latch on. Then she went looking for Norman. At least his body wasn't lying upside down on the floor, she thought worriedly, but where was he?

"Norman!" she wailed.

A slight scratching sound caught her attention and she sighed with relief as Norman appeared on top of the drapes in the living room, his green head peering over the curtain rod.

"Oh, thank goodness!" she said huskily. "I'm glad they didn't get you, baby."

He was looking around with unusual attention, and his body was faintly bowed, his whip of a tail half raised and threatening. She knew better than to try and handle him in that mood, so she talked soothingly to him and turned down the thermostat; she could lower his body temperature and pick him up easily, but it would take time.

She immediately packed a bag with what she would need for the night. No way was she going to stay in the apartment after what had happened. She knew she should call the police, but she was reluctant to: she had a terrible feeling that the break-in had something to do with Cousin Jenny, and the last thing she wanted was to put Jenny in danger. She might do that by involving the law enforcement people. And she knew from experience that Jenny had contacts of her own among the hush-hush government bureaus. She'd try to get in touch with Jenny and let her handle it.

When Norman was calmer, she got him down and put him in his cage, taking along his supper in a Baggie. The phone started to ring just as she left the apartment, but she didn't answer it. It might very well be the burglar or burglars to see if she was at home.

With a tiny shudder, she relocked the door, for all the good that would do, and left the building.

She and Norman spent a long night at a nearby Holiday Inn, with Norman irritable in his confined space. He wasn't used to being shut up, but she couldn't risk letting him out. He had a knack for wedging himself into tight places to keep from being moved somewhere else. She could remember having to have an appliance serviceman move the refrigerator to extricate Norman, who was coiled around the appliance's motor. The repairman, fortunately, was unique; he hadn't been afraid of giant lizards. The mechanic who'd had to get Norman out from under the front seat of her car, before she'd sold it and defected to public transportation, had broken out in a cold sweat while he worked and muttered something about retiring.

The next morning, she was hollow eyed and jumpy. She didn't like leaving Norman in her apartment alone, but maybe the unwelcome visitors wouldn't come back. She didn't know how she was going to face the weekend alone, watching the door all the time. Maybe she should buy a gun....

Sure, she thought as she locked Norman in the apartment and went to work. That was a great idea, considering that she was afraid of them and hated the noise. She'd probably shoot herself before she'd be able to shoot a burglar.

She hadn't put her hair up because she was too tired to care how it looked, and the dress she had on was of lavender cotton—and was wrinkled. She felt as bad as she looked, and God only knew what Mr. Ritter was going to say when he saw her.

In fact, he came out of his office looking almost as bad as she did. He, too, was rumpled and he needed a shave. He was in slacks and a short-sleeved white shirt, the shirt unbuttoned at the throat. It was one of the rare times Danetta had ever seen him that way, and she caught her breath at the sight of his muscular torso. His skin was olive and his arms were faintly hairy, like the chest she could glimpse under the thin fabric. He didn't wear an undershirt, and his body was as sensual as the eyes that went over her close-fitting, knee-length dress with its flattering belt.

"Where the hell were you last night?" he asked immediately, his blue eyes flashing. His wavy dark hair was disheveled, and she realized why he was so rumpled.

"Didn't you go home at all?" she countered, frozen beside her desk as she studied him.

"No, I didn't go home," he said shortly. "And apparently you had a long night, too, by the look of you."

"Yes, I did," she sighed wearily. "I hardly slept..."

"Undoubtedly." His lips twisted into a cold smile. "How was it?"

She blinked. Were they talking about the same thing? "I don't understand."

"Like hell you don't," he returned icily. "They say sex isn't good for a virgin the first time. Was it disappointing?"

Her eyes widened and she started to speak, aghast at the contempt and anger in his hard face.

Just as she opened her mouth, Ben came by the door, grinning from ear to ear. "Morning, glory," he said, blowing her a kiss. "See you at lunch! Morning, boss," he added to Cabe. "Don't be too hard on her, she had a rough time."

Ben waved and went down the hall while Cabe stood vibrating with rage, his face paling as he stared at Danetta with eyes that made her want to back away.

"Get your pad and come into my office," he said coldly. "Maybe we can get some work done, if you can keep your mind off lover boy."

He turned and went back into the plush confines of his office while Danetta tried to get herself together. He thought she'd spent the night with Ben! It was almost comical, especially after the way he'd been with her the day before.

She got her pad and pen and went into the office, but when she tried to explain, to tell him what had happened, he cut her off. He shaved while he dictated, then put on his tie and his jacket and combed his hair without looking at her.

"Got all that?" he asked finally. "Call Karol and tell her I'll pick her up at eleven-thirty for lunch, and cancel my afternoon appointments," he added. "I don't know if I'll get back afterward." He smiled at Danetta's embarrassment. "Didn't you know that people made love in broad daylight? I'm surprised."

She got up, shaky, and went back to her own office without a word. She worked through the morning without looking up, without saying anything to Cabe Ritter. It was all she could do to keep from bursting into tears.

"You'll have to have Meadows bring lunch in here," he said curtly when he was ready to leave. "You can't leave the phone. Those offshore people are going to call about the part they need expressed out there today." He paused at the door and his blue eyes sparkled with rage as he looked at her bent head. "Stay out of my office with him. The sofa isn't for afternoon romps."

She opened her mouth to speak, but he was gone. She picked up her dictionary and threw it at the door.

"You beast!" she raged, trembling, her voice thick with tears. "I hate you!"

Ben Meadows walked in, picked up the book and studied it. "You do?"

She cleared her throat and dabbed at the tears. "Sorry. The boss just left."

"So I gathered. Ready for lunch?"

"I can't go," she said miserably. "He says I have to stay by the phone."

"Oh." He blinked. "Well...suppose I bring you back something?"

"I don't really want anything, Ben," she said as she sat back down. "Thanks anyway."

He hesitated. "We could go out to supper..."

She shook her head. "I don't think so."

His eyes studied her intently. "Anything wrong?"

She looked up. She almost told him, but there was something in his face that made her hesitate. She forced a smile. "Why, nothing at all," she said.

He nodded, smiling back. "Okay. Uh, how's your iguana?"

She didn't remember telling him she had one, but maybe Cabe had. "He's fine, thanks. Have a nice lunch."

"Sure. Sorry you can't come with me. I'll grab a burger on the way. I've got an appointment at one. See you later."

"Okay."

Everybody was acting funny today, she thought, staring after Ben. She put her face in her hands. It had been a horrible night and an even worse morning. At least Mr. Ritter wouldn't be back. She could get her work done and dread the night. It was too far to go to her parents' house in Missouri and she had no close girlfriends except Jenny, who was somewhere in the southwest. She groaned inwardly. What a time to be all alone!

Lunch came and went. She drank two cups of black coffee and wished she'd had enough sense to pack a candy bar or something. She was starving. She guessed Mr. Ritter would be having caviar and lobster or something equally exotic, and she hoped he and his blonde choked on it. She bit her lower lip as she saw in her mind the erotic way he'd kissed Karol that day in the office. He was probably doing that and more right now.

She got up from her desk and went into his office, her eyes on the long sofa where he'd put her the day before. She could close her eyes and feel his hard mouth on her own, feel the banked down fever she'd raised in him. She leaned against the doorway with her arms crossed tightly over her breasts and tears stung her eyes. It had all gone wrong so quickly. She'd had no chance at all with him. He should never have touched her. He knew how green she was. Why had he kissed her that way, when he was only playing around?

"Nothing to do, Miss Marist?"

She stiffened at the deep, curt voice from behind. She moved back into her own office, avoiding looking directly at him. "I . . . thought you wouldn't be back," she stammered.

He studied her thoroughly, noting the traces of tears on her long eyelashes, pondering the way she'd been staring at his sofa.

All at once, he couldn't believe she'd been with Ben all night. Not when she had that tormented look on her face, not when she'd quite obviously been reminiscing about what they'd done on that sofa together the day before.

He caught her arm as she passed him and held her firmly, his thumb absently caressing through the thin sleeve. "Where were you last night, baby?" he asked softly.

The tone and the endearment broke down her cool reserve. "At a motel," she said brokenly. "With Norman. Somebody . . . somebody broke into my apartment . . . !"

"Oh, God." He gathered her into his arms, pressing her close while she cried. His big hand smoothed her hair, his face nuzzled her soft cheek. "It's all right. I'll take care of you. Put the phone on hold for a minute and lock the door. We'll talk."

"But we can't," she whispered, her soft gray eyes searching his. "That phone call . . ."

"I phoned them while I was at lunch," he said gently. He wiped away the tears. "Lock the door."

She did as he instructed and followed him into his office. She started to sit down in the chair, but he picked her up and sat down in his big desk chair with her in his lap, fitting her comfortably into the curve of his arm. He lit a cigarette.

Her wide gray eyes searched his while she tried to adjust to the sudden shift in their turbulent relationship.

"Tell me what happened," he said quietly.

She did, from the time she'd arrived at her apartment until she'd stuffed Norman into his travel carrier and left for the motel. "I don't even know what they were looking for," she said miserably. "But my apartment's a mess and I was so afraid."

"Why didn't you call me?" he asked.

She glanced up shyly. "I wanted to," she confessed. "But it didn't seem fair to involve you."

"I don't mind being involved. Could it be anything to do with Jenny's new project?" he asked.

"I thought about that," she said. "I don't know. It's very hush-hush." She searched his eyes. "Could you ask your father?"

"For all the good it will do, yes." He sighed heavily. "My God, I can't believe this. At least they struck when you weren't at home."

"Yes," she agreed, but Danetta was afraid they might try again when she was at home. She couldn't quite bring herself to say that. After all, what could he do? Stand guard over her? She couldn't put him in that position, it wasn't fair. He was only her boss.

"I thought you'd been with Ben," he said abruptly, staring down at her quietly. "That's why I was so hard on you this morning. I'm sorry."

Her fingers touched his jacket lightly and she gazed helplessly at his sensuous mouth. "I don't feel that way about Ben," she replied.

He liked the husky note in her voice. He bent and started to brush his mouth against hers, but she turned her face into his throat.

"Don't," she whispered unsteadily. "You've been with her."

His heart stopped and then started again. His chest lifted heavily against her breasts. "No, I haven't," he said gruffly. "Not in the way you mean." He tilted her eyes up to his. "Not ever in the way you mean. I said what I did to get back at you for what I thought you'd done."

It was something she shouldn't have said, but she couldn't regret it after he'd confessed, with his pale blue eyes cutting into hers like that. Her breath came in tiny jerks and she couldn't tear her gaze away from his.

"You don't remember, do you?" he asked softly. "I told you yesterday that I don't sleep with Karol. I meant it. I haven't slept with a woman since before Christmas."

She wanted to ask him why, she wanted to understand him so much better than she did. He'd told her that he wasn't really a womanizer, but she was far too shy to ask him personal questions, even when she was lying in his big arms.

"You aren't going to give yourself to Ben, are you?" he asked suddenly, his voice curt, his eyes demanding.

"No!" she burst out.

He sighed angrily and took a long drag from the cigarette, his eyes drawn to the faint lift of her breasts under the soft fabric as she tried to breathe. "I shouldn't give a damn," he muttered. "It's none of my business what you do when you're not in this office. But I do," he said huskily, lifting his eyes back to hers. "The thought of you with another man hurts me."

She stopped breathing for a second. "Why?"

"Don't you know?" He bent to her soft mouth. "I want you, honey," he breathed, parting her lips with tender expertise. "I want your first time to be with me...." His mouth moved slowly against hers, more deeply and hungrily by the instant, until the erotic pressure of it, added to the sweet, shocking words, brought her arms up around his neck.

He felt her response and his restraint was lost to the wind. He got rid of the cigarette, hoping he'd found the ashtray, and his big arms swallowed her. He nudged her lips apart and penetrated her mouth with his tongue in a rhythm that made her moan.

Kissing wasn't enough. He was burning. His hand slid up her rib cage to the curve of her breast and he lifted his head enough to see her eyes as he touched her there.

She stiffened a little, but she didn't stop his hand or say anything. His fingers moved slowly on her, the sound of them brushing against the fabric oddly loud in the quiet office.

"I can't remember a time when it was this exciting to touch a woman," he whispered, watching her responses as he moved closer and closer to the betraying hardness and felt her tremble with each slow caress. "It's all new to you, isn't it?"

"I never wanted anyone to do this to me," she managed shakily.

"Until now. With me." He built the excitement until she was moving against him, and his body responded instantly to the warm softness of her belly when he turned her and his hand suddenly moved completely over her breast.

She cried out. She hadn't meant to, but the fierce passion she felt was uncontrollable. Her hands dug into his nape and she shuddered as his hand caressed her.

"Baby," he whispered shakily. "Baby, I never realized... Kiss me," he breathed against her mouth as he lifted her closer. "Kiss me. Don't be afraid to let me show you how much I want you...."

She should have been, she thought with her last whisper of sanity, because his arousal was blatant and his hand was insistent at the base of her spine, moving her against him in a way that made her tremble. But she wasn't afraid of him. She registered his reaction to her with wicked delight, and when he started to unbutton her dress, her only thought was that it was going to be heaven to feel his hand against her soft skin.

He felt her tremble and loved her reactions, but things were rapidly getting out of hand. His own arousal was hurting him, and sanity seemed to fall on him like a wall. She was a virgin. This was his office, and it was in the middle of a business day. He lifted his head and looked down into her drowsy, hungry eyes, and he wanted to scream his frustration at the top of his lungs. Not here, he told himself firmly. Not now.

He took a slow breath and searched her eyes, his own dark blue with unsatisfied passion as they searched over her yielding body, her swollen lips, her adoring eyes.

"We can't make love like this," he said unsteadily. "My God, it's not possible. Not here."

"Make . . . love?" she echoed in a dazed tone.

He drew in a steadying breath, his face drawn and taut. His hand that had been holding her hips hard against his let go, and slid up her back. He shuddered faintly and put her away from him, helping her gently to her feet. His hands caught her arms and steadied her when she swayed.

"This won't do," he said heavily. "I really can't seduce you in my swivel chair during lunch. There's something in the office manual about that sort of thing, maybe we should both read it."

She heard the faint humor in his tone and smiled. "I guess so."

He tilted her eyes up to his. "I'm going out to Dad's for the weekend. Pack up your Irish lizard and I'll take you with me. My . . . half brother, Nicky, is a lizard freak," he said hesitantly. "You and he will get along fine."

So that was what he'd meant. She couldn't seem to get her mind to work. "But I can't go to your father's house with you," she said blankly. "I wasn't invited."

"You will be," he said with a rueful smile, still pale from the anguish of having to stop. "When he hears I've asked you, he'll hang from the chandelier and do a jig on the piano. He likes you." His mouth twisted wryly. "You're number one on his list of suitable candidates to marry me."

His, but not Cabe's, she thought sadly.

He read that expression quite accurately. His fingers touched her cheek, lightly brushing down to her mouth. "If I had a list," he said slowly, "I think you'd be number one on mine, too. You're very sweet to make love to."

"Along with dozens of others..." She tried to laugh it off.

His thumb pressed down over her lips, stifling the words. "I don't want anyone else," he said shortly. "Why in God's name do you think I've been celibate this long? Ever since I caught you under the mistletoe, I've dreamed of you every damned night. I can't even get in the mood with any other woman."

Her shocked eyes lowered to his chest while she let that sink in. She couldn't believe he meant it.

"I'm a playboy, isn't that what you think? A rounder who uses and discards women like paper napkins." He laughed shortly. "I'm as fastidious in my way as you are. Sex for its own sake never appealed to me."

She breathed unsteadily and her hands were cold where they rested on his jacket.

He groaned, pulling her hands under it to warm them against his rib cage. "I wish I could make you understand what it is to go hungry for someone."

"What makes you think I don't?" she asked huskily. Her eyes lifted slowly to his, and he read in them exactly what she was trying to say.

"Do you want me that way?" he whispered, awed by the faint adoration in her soft eyes.

She bit her lower lip. It was dangerous to admit it to him, to let him know, but it seemed the time for confidences. "Yes," she whispered back, her voice breaking.

His chest rose and fell heavily. His jaw tightened with the effort to control what he was feeling. He framed her face in his big, warm hands and brought it up to his.

"You're a virgin," he groaned at her lips. "My God, I can't...!"

He put her away from him again with a harsh curse and ran his hands roughly through his thick, wavy dark hair. He looked for the cigarette he'd discarded earlier and found it burned out in the ashtray. He lit another, fumbling with the lighter.

She stared at his broad back without moving, her arms locked around her chest, her heartbeat shaking her. It had been an altogether unexpected afternoon.

"I don't want to get married!" he ground out. He turned and glared at her. "And I'm not going to seduce you. Not if you strip naked and do a belly dance right here."

Her eyebrows shot up. He looked strange. "Well, I've never stripped in front of a man," she faltered. "And I can't belly dance."

"It was just a figure of speech." He sighed angrily. He lifted the cigarette to his lips and inhaled, watching her with hungry eyes. She was lovely, with her hair disheveled and her pretty mouth swollen from his kisses. His eyes lingered on her lips. "Did I bruise your mouth?" he asked huskily. "I didn't mean to."

"No, it's... all right," she stammered. She colored and avoided his piercing gaze. "I should go back to work."

"If you want to avoid being bent back over my desk and ravished, that might be a good idea," he said humorously.

She hesitated. "Are you angry?"

"I'm frustrated," he replied quietly. "I wanted you so much it hurts."

Her lips parted. "Oh. I'm sorry...!"

"Talking about it doesn't help." He gave her a rueful smile and went back to his desk. "Put the phone back on the hook and unlock the door. Maybe ten people will come in and we'll be too busy to look at each other until quitting time." He glanced back at her with eyes that almost burned. "I wasn't kidding," he said huskily. "I've heard of people making love on desks, and this one is plenty big enough. Stay out of here."

"Yes, sir," she said, her eyes helplessly adoring him.

"Those eyes," he groaned. He turned away to the window, shuddering. "Danetta, please, for God's sake, stop looking at me!"

"Yes, sir." She knew she sounded like a parrot, but it was fascinating to see him so vulnerable, and over her! She forced her legs to move back into her own office.

She replaced the phone and unlocked the door, but nobody came or called. So Cabe called someone and stayed on the phone until someone did come. Danetta went through the motions of working and tried not to think about the weekend and how she was going to survive being that close to Cabe without giving in to him. In his right mind, she knew he'd never come near her, as fanatical as he was about his freedom. But he seemed to be just as vulnerable as she was, and unless they had plenty of chaperoning, it was inevitable that something was going to happen. She wondered how she'd live with it if she gave in.

By the time five o'clock arrived, she was a seething mass of doubts and fears.

Cabe came out of his office putting on his jacket. He turned off the lights, his face like stone, his eyes glittering with blue fires.

"Get your coat, baby doll, and let's go," he said gently.

She closed up while he waited, watching her. When she turned back to him, his hand reached for hers and his fingers tangled gently into her own as he towered over her. Tingles of delicious feeling worked their way up her spine.

"Don't be afraid," he said quietly, looking down at her while they waited for the elevator. "I think I can keep my head. But you're coming with me. I won't leave you in your apartment alone."

"Your father..."

"...is delighted," he replied. "I phoned him before I came out of the office. Cynthia extended her own invitation. I'm not thrilled about your Irish lizard, but I guess a man can get used to anything," he finished wryly.

"He doesn't bite," she promised. "He's a vegetarian."

"If you say so." He sighed, closing his fingers more tightly around hers. His eyes slid up to hers, holding them. "Lock your bedroom door tonight," he whispered as the elevator approached. "You can't afford to trust me. Not the way I feel right now."

She started to speak, but the doors opened. He led her inside and didn't say another word until they were on the ground floor and headed out to his car. And then it was all business, as if he needed the diversion to keep his mind off her. She smiled to herself, wondering at the newness of what she felt, of what he seemed to feel. Please, she thought fervently, please let him love me.

Six

Cabe drove Danetta to her apartment, but he hesitated noticeably at her door.

"He isn't an attack lizard," she reassured him, because she knew why he was reluctant to go into the apartment. "It's all right."

He waited for her to open the door and then he stepped inside. Unfortunately Norman had just come out of the bathroom, and was in the hall that led to the living room. Norman was in a temper, and he wasn't used to men. He took one look at Cabe and bristled, twisting his body and dropping his dewlap and opening his pink mouth.

"My God!" Cabe backed out into the hall.

"Norman, you show-off!" Danetta sighed angrily. "Go on. Scoot!" She shooed him into the kitchen. He went, glancing over his shoulder at her as if she'd mortally offended him. She filled his food bowl and the dewlap went down as he began to eat shredded carrots and avocado.

"It's safe now!" she called to Cabe. "He's eating!"

He came into the apartment warily, his blue eyes narrowed and cautious as he searched for the iguana. "He doesn't like me," he said with pure irritation.

"He isn't used to men," she explained. "In fact, I don't think he's ever seen one, except for my father. He's nervous because he had a fright yesterday and then he got moved into a strange place last night and shut up. Iguanas are nervous creatures. He's really more frightened of you than you are of him."

He glared at her. "I'm not frightened of him," he said stiffly. "I just didn't want to rush him, that's all."

She smiled up at him. "He'll get used to you." She paused and cleared her throat. "For the weekend, I mean."

He studied her face for a long moment. "I expect to be around longer than a weekend, Danetta," he said quietly. "Much, much longer than that."

Her heartbeat seemed unusually loud as they looked at each other and she felt her knees going weak. "I don't know if I can handle an affair," she whispered.

"I don't know if I can, either," he replied huskily. "I've never had one."

"Never?" she asked, her eyebrows arching.

"Never. The occasional one-night stand, and once I thought I was in love when I was younger." He smiled gently. Then the smile faded. "But I've never felt like this with a woman. I don't quite know how to cope." His hands rested on her shoulders. "And to be blunt, that first time scares the hell out of me."

She searched his eyes, puzzled. "Why?"

"I told you I'm not a rounder." His broad shoulders lifted and fell. "I don't know a lot about virgins, and I've never had to hold anything back." His eyes held hers. "Restraint is difficult for a man after a long dry spell, you see." His hands contracted. "That's what it's going to mean if we have each other," he said curtly. "I'll have to hurt you. Deliberately. You understand?" He sighed roughly. "I don't know if I can."

She'd never considered that from a man's point of view, and it touched her that he cared about her comfort. She rested her forehead on his jacket, sighing because of the way he brought her close and held her so tenderly.

"I've always been a little afraid of it before," she confessed shyly. "But if it's uncomfortable, it will only be that once, and afterward..." She swallowed, her nails clinging to the smooth fabric of his jacket. "Afterward, you won't ever hurt me again, will you?"

His hands slid down her back, gently caressing. "Afterward," he whispered in her ear, "I'll arouse you very slowly and make the sweetest kind of love to you, and you'll go to sleep in my arms."

She shivered with the thought, closing her eyes as she clung to him. "I can't believe this is happening."

"If you want the truth, neither can I," he said gently. His lips brushed her forehead. "But I'm not sorry that it has. Are you?"

She looked up at him and shook her head. "No matter what happens, I'm not sorry."

He was breathing deliberately, his eyes frankly adoring. He let her go and moved back. "You'd better get your things together," he said. "They're expecting us by six."

"All right." She left him pacing the living room while she put what she'd need for a weekend into her suitcase. Then she went into the kitchen to pack Norman's snacks.

"What are you doing that for?" he asked, scowling as she took food out of the refrigerator.

"It's Norman's," she explained. "He likes quiche and spinach soufflé..."

"Oh, for God's sake, you don't need to carry food for him. Just tell Mrs. Fitchens what he eats and she'll fix it," he assured her.

She looked dubiously at Norman. "Does Mrs. Fitchens like lizards?"

"Not a lot," he replied. "My father told me that she went after one of Nicky's with a broom once when it got loose in her kitchen. She's mostly sane, but reptiles upset her. Thank God Nicky only likes lizards and not snakes."

"How old is Nicky?" she asked softly because she sensed the boy was a painful subject for him.

"Nicky is eight," he said quietly. He moved restlessly toward the living room. "Cynthia got pregnant the same year my mother died. It damned near killed me."

"I'm sorry," she said, moving close to him. She slid her arms around him and held him, laying her cheek against his hard chest. "You must have loved your mother very much."

"Too much," he said huskily. He wrapped Danetta up against him. "More than I was ever able to love Eugene. When she died, something died in me. Eugene was remarried in no time, and no sooner married than he was an expectant father. He couldn't have loved my mother and done that so quickly after she died."

"What's Nicky like?" she asked softly.

His body moved against hers as he shrugged. "I don't really know. We're not very close."

So that was what Eugene had meant when he said that Cabe hurt Nicky. Probably the boy worshiped him and didn't understand why his half brother resented him so much.

"But I do know that he likes lizards," he added on a laugh. "And frogs."

"I like frogs, too," she murmured.

"It figures." He drew away from her, frowning. "Why lizards? Why not something sensible, like a cat?"

"I'm allergic to fur," she said simply. "I wanted a pet and then I found Norman in a pet shop. He had an infected mouth and nobody else would bother trying to feed him. But I did. He must have liked me, because he lived. Mostly sick baby iguanas don't. They take a lot of special care."

He brushed back the hair from her face, his eyes soft on her beautiful complexion, her adoring gray eyes. "You're a giving person," he said quietly. "Be careful not to give too much."

"You can't give too much," she said. "Only not enough."

His expression began to close up.

"I didn't mean you, Cabe," she whispered, smiling up at him.

His body tingled with a myriad of confusing sensations. She appealed to him far too much. She made him hungry for that special warmth that she seemed to have for everything and everyone.

He took her by the waist and lifted her on a level with his eyes, muscles bulging under his jacket as he held her there with easy strength.

"I don't know if I like having my mind read," he murmured.

"Well, let me know when you decide," she said, smiling into his eyes. "You're very strong," she murmured, liking his strength.

"Working on oil rigs will make a man strong or break him." He brushed his mouth over hers. "I like carrying you around, Miss Marist. You don't weigh much, do you?"

"A little over a hundred and ten pounds," she protested. "I'm heavy."

He grinned, nuzzling her mouth with his. "No, you're not."

"You taste of cigarette smoke...."

"Do I?" His mouth hardened on hers and his arms slid around her, pulling her into a long, hungry embrace. She wondered why it felt so strange to be close to him, and then she realized that they'd never kissed each other standing up before. It had always been sitting down.

He let her slide down his body, against the arousal he couldn't help, and she moaned at the blatant hunger, at the sudden sharp pleasure she felt in her stomach.

"We haven't done it like this, have we?" he asked huskily, holding her hips to his with both hands, dragging her closer while he watched her react to him. "It's different this way."

"Yes," she groaned, helpless to keep her response from him. Her teeth ground together and she gave in to it, letting her body go limp, letting him lift her just enough to expertly fit her to the changed contours of his body. She cried out, a moan of helpless sound, and his hands contracted with bruising strength as he shuddered.

"Danetta," he whispered in anguish, his brows knitting as his mouth ground into hers. His hands lifted her into him rhythmically, so that the sensations quickly grew unbearable.

"Please," she whimpered into his mouth, shaking with the force of what he'd aroused in her. "Please, Cabe, please, please...!"

He heard her through a fog of helpless need. He was almost too far gone to stop. His hands let go and she dropped to the floor, feeling boneless. He caught her in time to spare her a fall, and she looked up into his stony features with dazed wonder.

"We've got to stop this," he bit off. "Inevitably I'm going to lose it."

NO COST! NO OBLIGATION TO BUY! NO PURCHASE NECESSARY!

PLAY "LUCKY 7"
AND GET AS MANY AS SIX FREE GIFTS...

HOW TO PLAY:

1. With a coin, carefully scratch off the silver box at the right. This makes you eligible to receive one or more free books, and possibly other gifts, depending on what is revealed beneath the scratch-off area.

2. You'll receive brand-new Silhouette Desire® novels. When you return this card, we'll send you the books and gifts you qualify for *absolutely free*!

3. Unless you tell us otherwise, every month we'll send you 6 additional novels to read and enjoy. If you decide to keep them, you'll pay only $2.24* per book—that's 26¢ less per book than the cover price—plus only 69¢ postage and handling for the entire shipment.

4. When you subscribe to Silhouette Reader Service™, we'll also send you additional free gifts from time to time, as a token of our appreciation for being a home subscriber.

5. You must be completely satisfied. You may cancel at any time simply by writing "cancel" on your statement or returning a shipment of books to us at our cost.

Business Reply Mail

No Postage Stamp
Necessary if Mailed
in Canada

Postage will be paid by

SILHOUETTE BOOKS
P.O. Box 609
Fort Erie, Ontario
L2A 9Z9

Canada Post
Postes Canada
125

"If I feel like that when you do, I won't even know if you hurt me," she whispered shakily.

He drew in a slow breath, bristling with pride and delight. "We'd better go, little one."

"All right." She moved away from him reluctantly, her face flaming as she remembered how intimate they'd been for those few turbulent minutes. "I'll pack up Norman."

"This I've got to see," he murmured, and moved to the counter to watch.

It wasn't that difficult. Danetta simply picked him up and put him in the cage on his hot-rock, careful not to catch his elegant tail in the door. He had to lie on the hot-rock to help him digest his food. She fastened it and Norman flattened on the floor, closing his eyes.

"He goes to sleep when he's been fed," she told Cabe. "Isn't he cute?"

He raised an eyebrow. Cute wasn't a word he thought of in connection with the lizard. "Let's go," he said. He was still having a few problems with his body, which he hoped he could get under control before he and Danetta got to the ranch.

Eugene and Cynthia lived northwest of Tulsa in Orange County a few miles from Keystone Lake—one of six huge man-made lakes within an hour of Tulsa in the area known as "green country." Fishing was big business around there, and bait and tackle shops were prolific, along with the ever-present mule-head oil wells pumping merrily away.

"Isn't there an old oil field around here somewhere?" she murmured, looking out the window.

"Plenty. We were on top of a pre-World War I field down at Beggs when we talked to Harry Deal," he reminded her. "A lot of drillers are opening up old wells with new hopes. Sometimes it pays off. My father's about to open up one of his old ones just for kicks. Not that he needs the money," he added dryly.

"I can believe that." Her eyes caught a sign as they left the city and she smiled. "Why is Tulsa called Tulsa, do you know?" she asked. "I've never noticed, but it sounds sort of odd."

"I was just reading an article about Tulsa in an old *National Geographic*. They say the name dates back to Alabama, in fact," he told her, taking a draw from his cigarette as he drove. "Tulsey was what the Lochapoka Indians called their village in Alabama. According to some sources it's a corruption of a Creek word for Old Town—Tallassee. They brought the ashes from their sacred fire to Oklahoma back in the nineteenth century and rekindled the fire under an oak tree—I think I've pointed out the tree to you, it's fenced in. Anyway, that's where the name Tulsa came from."

"There were a lot of Indians here."

"Point of fact, until Oklahoma became a state in 1907, three sovereign Indian nations converged here—the Creeks, the Cherokee and the Osage," he told her. "And the word Oklahoma is Choctaw—it means 'red people.'"

She studied him closely. "I don't suppose you have any Indian blood?"

"Because I'm blue eyed?" he mused, glancing at her. "Don't you believe it. I have cousins who are Osage and Arizona Apache."

She looked down at her hands, thinking about children. God knew why. If he had children, they'd have an interesting heritage.

"It would rain today," he murmured, watching the beginning of a storm sprinkle down on the windshield. He turned the wipers on. "Dad has a sailboat. I thought we might go sailing, but if this goes on all weekend, there won't be a chance."

"Downpours and drought and tornadoes," she shook her head. "At least the weather is never boring here."

"That's a fact." He smiled at her. "Dad told Nicky about your ugly friend back there. He's excited about seeing a real live iguana."

"Norman isn't ugly," she defended her pet. "He's..." She thought for a word.

"Ugly," he supplied.

"To him, we probably are," she said finally.

"No doubt."

She let her eyes run slowly over his profile with pure delight. "Do you know how to sail?" she asked.

He chuckled. "I learned when I was just a boy. I got wet a lot first," he added, "but eventually I got the hang of it. I like to fish, too. Do you?"

"Just with a standard rig," she qualified. "I used to go fishing with my granddad when I was a girl."

"This is a great place for it. What else do you like to do?"

"Ride bikes, play baseball, climb mountains," she said shyly. "We lived in the Ozarks. It's so beautiful."

"Indeed it is. I like baseball myself, although I'm getting to the age where making the bases in a hurry isn't quite as easy as it was." He scowled faintly as he crushed out his cigarette in the ashtray and then gave her a brief, intent scrutiny. "Those thirteen years may matter to you one day."

Her heart skipped, but she didn't avert her eyes. "They'll never matter to me," she said quietly. "Not ever, Cabe."

He reached over and caught her hand, holding it tightly in his. He didn't say anything. He didn't have to. The look on his face said it all.

The ranch was near Keystone Lake in a sparsely wooded area with plenty of pasture for Eugene's horses and pure-bred Santa Gertrudis cattle. It was close enough to the main highway, but far enough back that the traffic wasn't a nuisance. The lake was a silver streak in the distance, over the undulating pasture.

Eugene came out to meet them. Behind him was a big gray, modern house with lots of windows and a balcony, and two huge decks leading off the sides. Oak trees shaded it. There was a swimming pool visible in back of the house, as well as a garage and tennis court.

"It's very pretty," Danetta sighed.

"The house is only a few years old," he told her, his expression becoming hard as he added, "he tore down the other one where I was born, and put this one up instead."

Her fingers tightened on his. "Maybe he thought a clean break with the past was best for Cynthia."

"So it was. But not for me. I don't find it that simple to give up my memories."

Eugene was wearing jeans and a checked shirt, and he was all smiles as Cabe opened Danetta's door and helped her out. The old man clearly approved of her lavender dress, even with the faint wrinkles.

"Glad you could come," Eugene told her. "I'm sorry about the circumstances," he added quietly. "Cabe told me you'd had a break-in."

"Find out anything?" Cabe asked his father as he took Danetta's suitcase out of the car and propelled her toward the house.

"Not yet," Eugene said. "I've got my feelers out. We'll find the culprits. Enough about that. Let's get in out of the rain."

"Mist more than rain," Cabe remarked as they walked up onto the front porch. "It was pouring when we left Tulsa."

"It's spring," Eugene reminded him. "Thank your lucky stars you didn't run into a tornado along with the rain. They've had two already down around the state capitol."

Eugene opened the front door just as Danetta remembered another case that Cabe had left in the car.

"Norman!" she exclaimed. "We forgot him!"

"I was trying to," Cabe began.

"I'll get him," she said, rushing back out to the car.

"Norman?" Eugene asked with a frown.

"Don't ask," Cabe told him.

Danetta was back in seconds with Norman in his cozy carrying case in one hand. "Here he is."

Eugene peered through the wire door and his eyebrows arched. "That's an iguana, all right."

Danetta grinned. "His name is Norman and he's three years old."

Eugene stuck his hands into his pockets with a sigh. "Well, he'll feel right at home. Nicky's got everything except an iguana—"

"Is she here? Did she bring it?" an excited voice demanded, and a young boy came out onto the porch. He was the image of Cabe, already tall for his age, dark-haired and blue eyed. He grinned up at Danetta. "You must be Dan. I'm Nicky. Is that your iguana? Can I see him?"

She burst out laughing. His excitement was contagious. "Yes, I'm Dan," she said, not even minding being called that for once. "And this is Norman."

He bent, looking through the cage. His head raised briefly as he looked up at Cabe. "Hi," he said with a shy, hopeful smile, but Cabe turned his attention to his father and ignored him. The light seemed to go out of the boy as he looked back at Norman.

An elegant woman of forty wearing designer jeans and a pink knit top came out onto the porch, smiling at the commotion. She had blond hair done up in a French twist, and her complexion was as fair as Eugene's was dark. Her eyes were dark and soft as they rested on the boy.

"He likes things with warts and long tails," she explained to Danetta in a soft, sweet tone. "I'm Cynthia, and you must be Danetta. I'm glad to meet you at last. I've heard a lot about you."

"Was any of it repeatable?" Danetta asked the older woman with a smile.

"You'd be surprised," Cynthia said wickedly. "Hello, Cabe. It's good to see you."

Cabe nodded. He was looking at Nicky with hard eyes. Cynthia noticed and shooed everyone inside the house.

"I'll bring coffee and cake," she said. "Have you two eaten?"

"No," Cabe said.

"How about some sandwiches? Mrs. Fitchens had to go away for the weekend so we haven't eaten, either. I can slice some ham . . ."

"May I help?" Danetta offered. "Since I'm adding to the food problem, I can at least help solve it."

Cynthia took her arm and drew her along to the kitchen. "Yes, you may. Nicky, don't open the iguana's cage yet," she called back. "Wait until you and Danetta can take him out to the garage."

"Okay, Mom." The boy was sprawled on the floor, talking to Norman through the wire door.

"He doesn't bite," Danetta assured Cynthia.

"Oh, I'm used to lizards," Cynthia said easily. "I find them fascinating. Now tell me about your job. I do miss mine—I used to work for Eugene, you see." She sighed as she put out the ham and began to carve it. "Now I spend my life doing all sorts of volunteer work and taking on social projects and being here for Nicky. I don't need to work anymore, but having money can be rather confining sometimes. Some people have a hard time getting past the checkbook to the person, if you see what I mean," she added with a grin.

Danetta liked her already. She perched on a stool, putting mayonnaise and lettuce on bread for Cynthia. "I like working for Cabe," she replied. "Well, not all the time. He has a terrible temper..."

"Yes, I know," Cynthia mused. "He and his father don't get along very well." Her lovely face stilled. "He resents me, you see. I can't even blame him. Gene and I did rush it a bit, but I was so much in love, for the first time in my life. We got married and I was pregnant, and Cabe seemed to close the door on all of us."

"Tragic for all of you," Danetta said, her voice quietly sympathetic.

Cynthia turned. "Yes, it was. Cabe needs so badly to be a part of us, part of our family. Nicky worships him, but Cabe has no time for his half brother. Nicky is his biggest sore spot."

"Nicky looks just like him," Danetta sighed. "Or he will, in a few years."

"He favors Gene, just as Cabe does," Cynthia said with a wistful smile. "I thought the resemblance might do the trick, but it never has. In some ways, it's made it worse."

"Maybe it will change someday."

"I've hoped that it would for eight years," Cynthia replied. "I've given up. I'm glad you came with Cabe. This is the first time he's ever brought anyone with him."

"It was kind of him," she said gently. "I was really afraid to stay at my apartment, and motels aren't much more secure. I still don't know what they were after."

"Don't worry about it. All that clandestine stuff Gene's into makes me nervous, too." She passed a platter of sliced ham to Danetta and watched her put it on the bread. "Do I give you separate bedrooms?"

It was a simple question, but it got a very complex reaction. Danetta went scarlet and the look she gave Cynthia made the older woman burst out laughing.

"Oh, my," she mused. "Poor Cabe. I take back the question and the implication. I'm delighted to know there are women like you left in the world. Of course, we're very much in the Bible Belt here, so maybe our attitudes are different from that of other places."

Danetta smiled shyly. "I do have company. Two girls I know in other departments at work are from Georgia and New Jersey, respectively, and they're just as old-fashioned as I am. It isn't all a question of geography, I guess," Danetta returned. She shifted restlessly on the stool and finished arranging the platter of sandwiches. "I'm sorry I look so disreputable. I had to take my dress to the motel last night, and it looks as if I slept in it."

"If you'd like to change, we can eat later."

"No, that's perfectly all right," Danetta assured her. "I'm starved," she confessed. "I didn't have lunch!"

"Oh, you poor thing! I'll call the men and we'll sit right down," Cynthia said, and minutes later, they were eating.

It was a pleasant meal, except that Cabe ignored Cynthia and Nicky and talked almost exclusively to Eugene. Danetta talked about clothes to Cynthia and herpetology to Nicky, and they got along fine.

After they were through, Danetta went up to the pretty white-and-blue room Cynthia had given her and changed into jeans and a yellow knit sweater so that she and Nicky could take Norman out to the garage.

It was a big place, with a huge den off the main garage and a bedroom upstairs.

"This is where Dad's houseman used to live," Nicky explained to Danetta after they'd left the others behind and were on their way through the misty rain. "But he quit and so there's nobody right now. That's why I get to use it for my pets. Here they are."

He pointed to a whole shelf of aquariums that had been converted into habitats for various amphibians and reptiles. There was a huge, enclosed wire cage, complete with fresh water and a food dish.

"That's for Norman," Nicky told her. "Dad built it for Mr. Bunny, but Mr. Bunny died last summer. I thought it would make a nice place for an iguana to spend the night."

"And so it would." Danetta smiled. "Here, let's put him in."

"Could I hold him?" Nicky asked hopefully.

"Sure." She said it with reservation because Norman wasn't used to males. But when she took him out and put him gently in Nicky's hands, so that his belly was supported, he half closed his eyes and stared up at the boy with no sign of irritation or fear.

"Wow!" Nicky chuckled. "Wow, isn't he neat?"

"I think so," Danetta told him. "I've had him for three years. He eats quiche and pizza and all sorts of things iguanas aren't supposed to like, and sometimes he'll come when I whistle."

"He's an iguanid," Nicky said authoritatively. "So are anoles, you know. I have six, two males and four females, but I have to cage the males separately because they fight."

"I like anoles. Yes, I know they're classified in the class of reptilia and order squamata—which doesn't include crocodiles, beak-heads and turtles—but in the suborder sauria, which excludes snakes. Genus," she added, grinning at Nicky, "is iguana. So the common green iguana—" she pointed at Norman "—is iguana iguana iguana."

"Very good!" Nicky returned. "You forgot chordata."

She clapped her hand over her mouth. "Sorry."

"Chor...what?" Cabe asked with a frown as he and Eugene and Cynthia joined them.

"Chordata," Nicky told him. "The kingdom is animalia, the phylum is chordata—having backbones. We're classifying Norman."

"Do tell?" Cabe murmured, keeping his distance from the reptile in Nicky's arms. "He seems to like you."

"Yes, doesn't he?" Nicky sighed. "I wish I could have one."

"Why can't you?" Eugene asked.

"Pet shops don't keep them. They say the babies don't live without a lot of care."

"Have Mr. Harris special order you one. I'll foot the bill for the air delivery," Eugene said.

"You mean it?" Nicky gasped. "Wow, thanks, Dad! Dan, can you teach me how to take care of him?"

"You bet," she said, smiling at him.

"Want to hold him, Cabe?" Nicky asked.

Cabe backed up another step without being obvious. "Not really, thanks. He's already done his smoking dragon imitation for me once today," he added with a faint smile.

"He thought you were an intruder," Danetta told him. "I'll bet he did that when the burglar came into the apartment, if he was on the floor. He might have bitten him if he'd come too close," she added thoughtfully, "or at least lashed him with his tail."

"I thought you swore he didn't bite," Cabe reminded her.

"Well, not normally," she qualified. "Any animal will bite if it's threatened."

"That's right," Nicky agreed. "My little anoles will bite if they're squeezed, and they're the sweetest little guys."

Danetta put Norman in the big cage, promising him supper, and then looked at Nicky's collection of anoles and frogs. The anoles looked like miniature crocodiles, and they changed color—living up to their nickname of "new world chameleons." They looked a lot like Norman had as a baby, but they were barely six inches long and full grown. The frogs were fascinating. He had a White's frog from Australia—a beautiful blue-green frog with huge eyes and suction-pad toes. He had a red-and-black poison arrow frog, Chinese painted frogs, fire-bellied toads and a huge bufo marinus, the biggest frog in the world. The bufo was highly toxic, like the poison arrow frog.

"That's quite a collection, Nicky," she mused.

"It took a long time to build," he said importantly. "I take care of them all by myself."

"And very well," she replied. "Don't you think so, Cabe?" she added with a pleading glance at the tall man beside her.

He sighed at the look in her eyes and averted his glance to an expectant Nicky. He smiled warmly for the first time. "Yes. I think you do very well, Nicky," he replied.

The change in the boy was miraculous. He seemed to glow. "Thanks, Cabe," he mumbled with faint embarrassment and began to rattle off the genealogy of the White's frog.

Danetta's eyes were on Cabe. He was watching Nicky, but now the hostility wasn't quite as noticeable. There was hope, she thought, that one day he could accept the boy. She'd do her part to help. Nicky needed Cabe. And whether or not he realized it, Cabe needed Nicky.

She slid her hand into Cabe's unobtrusively, feeling him stiffen and glance down quickly, frowning.

The reaction she got unnerved her, and she tried to draw her hand away. But his fingers tightened and he searched her eyes. Then he smiled, and all her doubts fell away. She moved a step closer and had to drag her attention back to Nicky, who was explaining the proper way to handle the toxic frogs and toads without risking exposure to the dangerous neurotoxins that they emitted. Cabe smiled at her, and she felt as if she'd swallowed warm wine.

Seven

———

Danetta learned more about Cabe in that one afternoon and evening than she'd found out in two years. She saw his diploma from high school and his bachelor's degree from Yale in business. She saw his trophies in riding competition and his shirt with the shirttail cut out that marked the day he flew solo in his airplane—and she hadn't even know that he could fly, because he didn't these days.

From Eugene she learned of Cabe's interest in Western history and his contributions to a scholarship in the arts for two students a year at the University of Oklahoma in Norman.

And while he might not be a reptile man, he had a keen interest in quarter horses and was an expert rider. Nicky told her that, with quiet pride in the half brother he saw so rarely.

While she was finding out things about Cabe from his family, he was on the phone trying to sort out an emergency at the company. The part had been flown out to the oil rig in the Gulf, but it had been the wrong part. The warehouse had mixed up the numbers and heads were rolling right and left. Cabe had to order two employees back to work to straighten things out, and the part was sent and installed without another hitch.

"I hate the equipment business," Cabe muttered as he rejoined the rest of them in the living room much later. He was in his socks, his jacket and tie off, his shirt half unbuttoned and rumpled. He looked... incredibly masculine, Danetta thought. He was a hairy man, but not offensively so, and that curling thatch on his chest made her fingers itch. She could hardly take her eyes off him.

He noticed her rapt stare with a faintly arrogant smile. He liked that shy appraisal. He sat down beside her on the sofa and slid a possessive arm over the back so that it rested almost touching her shoulder. Eugene and Cynthia exchanged amused glances.

"If you really hate the equipment business, come back and work for me," Eugene murmured dryly.

"No deal. I like what I do too much." Cabe glanced down at Danetta, his eyes soft and quiet. "Besides, you'd have me out of town all the time. I'm getting to the age where I'd like to stay in one place."

"We could work something out."

Cabe dragged his eyes away from the warmth in Danetta's and looked at his father. "No."

Eugene shrugged. "Okay. No harm in trying. Anybody want to watch that new science-fiction movie I bought?" He held it up and Danetta grinned from ear to ear.

"Like science-fiction, do you?" Cabe asked as Eugene put it on, and his arm drew her close.

"A lot," she whispered, bright with the joy she was feeling. It was incredible to be sitting here, with Cabe's arm around her, on the receiving end of that soft, smoldering look that had once frightened her.

"So do I," he murmured, brushing her lips with his in a soft, delicate kiss.

She couldn't believe that he'd done that, with his whole family present. It was almost a statement of intent. But he had, and while they watched the movie, he watched her.

He drew her hand slowly inside his open shirt and pressed it gently against his warm, hard chest, nestling it into the thick, curling mat of hair. He watched her try to disguise her reaction to the intimacy, smiling when her breath came jerkily and her eyes darted to the rest of the Ritter clan.

She needn't have worried. Eugene and Cynthia were cuddled together on the love seat nearest the television and Nicky was sprawled on his belly on the carpet. Nobody paid the least attention to Cabe and Danetta, which was a good thing because while Cabe coaxed her hand over his hard chest, his free hand was under her arm, blatantly teasing the curve of her breast.

I'll kill you, she thought through an agony of desire. I'll wrap your fishing rod around your neck and strangle you. Trying to sit still and not let hunger show was incredibly difficult. She almost groaned out loud as his long fingers brushed back and forth, back and forth on the soft curve under her arm. In no time, she was leaning heavily against his side, her own arm moving inconspicuously to give him enough room, her body helplessly lifting with the caress and coaxing him toward the hard, aching tip...

"How about some coffee?" Cabe asked suddenly, moving his arm as he stood. "Danetta and I will make it," he added when Cynthia reluctantly started to move.

"Want us to pause the film?" Eugene asked mischievously.

"No need. We'll catch up," Cabe returned. He had Danetta by the arm, propelling her quickly out of the room and down the hall. In the kitchen, he pushed through the swinging door and backed her up against the refrigerator, his arms catching his weight as he bent toward her. "Finally," he whispered huskily as he bent to her mouth. "My God, I couldn't have lasted much longer...!"

As his mouth covered hers, his hand glided over her breast completely, claiming it with expert tenderness. Danetta moaned and lifted her arms around him, welcoming his weight, his hunger. Mindlessly she kissed him back while the hum of the refrigerator and the soft whir of the ice maker running inside it barely covered the heavy sigh of Cabe's breathing and the beat of her own heart.

He lifted his head and pulled her arms from around him, sliding her cool hands over his chest. "That's good," he breathed, looking down at them. "Here." He unbuttoned the rest of his shirt and pulled it free of his slacks, guiding her hands over the hair-roughened warmth of tanned muscle, showing her how to touch him. "I hope you like hairy men, little one," he said huskily, "because I'm like my chest all over."

"I do," she choked, lifting her eyes to his. "I thought I'd die in there," she said jerkily.

"So did I." He slid his hands under her yellow knit sweater and grazed over the soft fabric of her bra, watching her body jerk at the unfamiliar caress. "I won't hurt you," he said quietly. "Does this lacy thing fasten in front or in back?"

"In...back."

He smiled gently. "Waste of time to wear it," he whispered, bending his head as his fingers found the catch and expertly undid it. Then his hands slid around her rib cage, his thumbs edging up, arousing, teasing, so that she gasped involuntarily and lifted toward them. "Want my hands on you?" he breathed into her mouth.

"Cabe," she sobbed. Her fingers grabbed his wrists and pulled them toward her.

"Easy now," he said softly. He lifted his head, looking down at her, pure pleasure in his eyes. "No, don't fight what you're feeling," he coaxed when she tried to back away, to get free of the desire that was heating up even as she fought it. His hands moved slowly on her, insistent, devastating. If it hadn't been for the refrigerator, she knew she'd have sunk to the floor.

"Oh…Cabe," she moaned, arching. "Make it…stop."

He nibbled her top lip gently. "Is it bad?" he whispered softly. "Do you ache?"

"Yes…!"

"So do I, precious girl," he breathed against her lips. "Try not to cry out when you feel my mouth."

She didn't understand until he pulled up her top and his mouth closed on her breast. She hadn't expected anything quite so intimate, and when she felt the warm moist suction and looked down at the dark head against her breast, she shuddered all over with the force of her feelings.

"Cabe!"

Her voice didn't sound like hers. It was wild and high-pitched and shaky. Her hands caught jerkily in his hair, pulling him closer while a white-hot streak of pleasure shot from her breast down into her belly and set her on fire with the need for him.

"Not so hard, sweetheart," he whispered as he lifted his head and looked into her frantic eyes. "You're delicate here." He cupped her breast gently, his thumb smoothing slowly over the taut nub. "I don't want to bruise you with my teeth."

She managed to drag in a breath and gazed at him in wonder. His eyes were dark and glittery as he looked at her pretty breasts with their pink tips so hard and dusky.

"I didn't know how beautiful a woman could be until now," he whispered softly. "I've never had a virgin, Danetta," he breathed as his mouth smoothed with exquisite tenderness over her high breasts. "I don't know if I can live through the pleasure of having you...."

She only half heard him. Her lips touched his dark hair gently while she stood trembling under the force of all the new sensations racking her slender body. His hands brushed over her bareness with tender, searching motions, adoring her while his mouth lifted back to cover hers. He moved so that one powerful leg eased between both of hers, and he let her feel him in an intimacy that destroyed what little was left of her self-control.

Her hands slid down his back, savoring the hard muscles, and onto his hips. He was powerfully built, muscles as hard as rock supporting that big frame. She loved touching him.

"Lower," he said against her mouth. "Don't stop there."

She swallowed, her eyes straining to see his. "I can't...touch you that way."

"Yes, you can." His hands caught hers and pulled them to the back of his thighs, smoothing them upward. "Pull me to you and hold me there," he whispered. "There's nothing to be frightened of. We both know I'm aroused, but I can't very well take you here."

"It will hurt you," she whispered brokenly, obeying him even as she said it.

He smiled through waves of desire. "No, it won't." He bent to her mouth again and his own hands went to her hips, sliding them sensuously against his own so that the throbbing warmth of his body was reflected in hers, so that she could hardly breathe for the ache he kindled.

"If we were alone, I wouldn't stop," he whispered against her trembling lips. "I'd peel those jeans off and unfasten my belt, and we'd make love right here."

Tears stung her eyes because she knew she'd welcome it. He knew it, too. He lifted his head and looked down into her soft gray eyes, which were brimming with tears.

"You'd give in to me if I asked you, wouldn't you?" he murmured, his voice deeper than usual, full of warmth.

"Yes."

His hands slid down over her breasts, over the soft swell of her hips. His eyes held hers while he fought for control. "What if I asked you to come to me tonight, when everyone is asleep?"

She bit her lower lip until it almost bled, trying to stall until her body stopped screaming for him.

He tapped her cheek gently. "Don't scar your lip. I won't ask you to sleep with me. Not yet, anyway." He moved away from her enough to refasten her bra and rearrange her top. His hands were deft, if a little unsteady. He smiled at her faint embarrassment. "Men and women have been pleasuring each other like this since the beginning of time. We didn't do enough to weigh down your conscience." He nuzzled his face into her throat. "I can think of a few things I'd like to do, though. Want to hear them?"

"No."

"Yes, you do." He whispered them into her ear, feeling her squirm and make protesting little noises. He lifted his head and chuckled with pure delight at the color in her face. "You wouldn't like to do that with me?" he taunted.

She pushed at his chest. "You're a beast," she muttered, but her shy smile gave her away.

"I'm a hungry beast," he replied, wrapping her up tight in a bear hug, but without any sexual message behind it. He kissed her pert nose, liking the way her curly hair floated over her shoulders and the sweet, womanly smell of her body in his arms. "Suppose we make that coffee and slice some of Cynthia's cake?"

She smiled. "Okay." Hesitantly she reached up to his face. He caught her fingers to his lips and then gave them free license to touch him, to explore his hard features.

"What are we going to do if you fall in love with me?" he asked softly, and not as if the thought bothered him at all.

She felt her heart jump, but she wasn't going to be trapped with such a question. "We might have to shoot me," she said. "Or is that if I break a leg?" She frowned thoughtfully.

He smiled at her, looking years younger and more re-laxed than she'd ever seen him. "You look loved. When we get back in there, Eugene's going to grin his head off."

"You dragged me in here—" she began.

His eyebrows arched. "Me?" he interrupted. "My God, you were the one making roads in the hair on my chest. What was I supposed to do, sit there and let you torture me to death?"

She glared at him. "And just what were you doing while I was torturing you?" she demanded, sticking her fingers into his chest.

He pursed his lips and dropped his gaze to her breasts. "Getting an education on how virgins react to a sensual touch."

She whistled through her teeth. "Naughty, naughty."

"You were the one trying to get me to move my hand closer to your..."

"Let's make some coffee!" she burst out.

He let her go, chuckling at her high color. While she found the pot and the coffee canister and the filters, he stood against the refrigerator with his arms folded across his chest, looking rakish and deliciously handsome. She glanced at him, with helpless appreciation, smiling when he caught her.

"You...look a little rakish," she murmured.

"Is that a subtle hint that I need to button my shirt and tuck it back in so that Cynthia and Gene won't suspect that we've been making love to each other in their kitchen?" he asked innocently.

"If the way your father looked at us when we left was any indication, he could probably give you a play-by-play of everything we did."

He chuckled, fishing in his pocket for a cigarette. "No doubt about that." He lit it and blew out a cloud of smoke. "I'd quit, except that this is so damned pleasurable after..." He stopped.

She paused with the coffee in one hand and looked at him, puzzled by the sudden stop. Then it dawned on her what he was going to say. That smoking was so pleasurable after he'd made love to a woman. She wasn't the first woman he'd done this, and more, with. And that brought back a lot of unpleasant memories.

She turned away and put on the coffee without another word. The beautiful harmony had gone, dashed away by bitter reality.

He came up behind her with a heavy sigh, his hands resting lightly on her shoulders. "I can't erase the past, as much as I might want to," he said after a minute. "But I meant it about my reputation. I'm not the playboy I let you think I was. It's important to me that you believe what I'm telling you."

She looked up at him. "Why?" she asked gently, her gray eyes worried. "I'm just an interlude..."

His lips brushed hers, stopping the words. "I don't treat interludes the way I've treated you tonight," he said, quietly serious. "And I think you know it."

She drew in a ragged breath. "I'm so afraid," she whispered, voicing her doubts as she searched his pale blue eyes.

"That makes two of us, honey," he replied surprisingly. "Commitment is the boogeyman to me. It's something I've never wanted." He searched her eyes, then let his gaze move down to her swollen lips, her firm little chin. "But I don't want an affair with you. I don't want other men touching you."

"I don't want other women touching you," she said hesitantly, and lowered her eyes to his bare chest.

He laughed bitterly. "My God, we're getting in over our heads, aren't we? A few kisses, and the world closes in. I didn't have any idea it would be like this."

"We could stop," she whispered without lifting her head.

"How?" he ground out. "Feel this!" He drew her hand to his chest and positioned it flat over his heart so that its heavy, hard beat shook her fingers. "Have you ever tried to stop a tornado? Because that might be easier. Unless you want to move to Siberia or Alaska and change your name, I don't think we can stop it. Even then, I'd find you," he said in a hunted undertone. His fingers contracted over hers, moving them on his hot skin. "I'd find you wherever you went. I'd have to."

"Why?"

"Because half a man can't live," he bit off against her mouth as he took it.

She melted into his body with the touch of his lips on her own, giving in as naturally as she breathed. She also felt that way about him, as if she'd lose half of herself if she lost him. But it wouldn't last. Despite his assertions that he wasn't promiscuous, he'd had his share of women, and they'd all been beautiful. Danetta had no illusions about her looks; she was passable, but she was never going to be a great beauty. He'd tire of her. She was just a novelty, that was all.

But she wanted him. She loved him. He wanted her, and if that was all she could have, all right. She slid her arms under his shirt and around his body, feeling his muscles tense, feeling him arch against her in a taut fever. In seconds he was aroused all over again, and this time she moved toward his body instead of trying to withdraw, loving the vivid evidence of his need for her.

"Not afraid of me now?" he whispered with rough humor.

"No," she whispered back.

His hands slid low on her spine and pushed her hips against his in slow, sensuous motions that made her teeth clench with pleasure.

"We're good together," he said unsteadily. "In bed, we'll satisfy each other so completely that neither one of us will ever be able to make love with anyone else. And that," he added, "is what scares the hell out of me."

Because he didn't want commitment, she supposed. She laid her cheek against his chest. "We don't have to go to bed together."

"Have you by any chance gone numb?" he asked, dragging her hips against his. "Just how long do you think I'm going to be able to control this?"

"I'll get pregnant," she mumbled, and then blushed when she realized what she'd said.

He laughed. His chest shook with it. He pushed her away with rough affection and lifted his burning cigarette to his lips.

"Damn you," he chuckled. "That wasn't fair."

"Yes, it was," she replied. "And I would. I know a lot of women are on the Pill, but I'd have to go to my family doctor to get it and he'd make me feel terrible. Or I'd have to go to a clinic, and sure as the world, I'd meet one of the ladies from my church going there for some other reason. I couldn't. I just couldn't."

He tugged a long lock of her curly hair. "I can understand that," he said.

Her eyes searched his longingly. "There are only a few hours a month when a woman can get pregnant."

"Don't you bet on it." He tapped her on the nose. "I remember reading that sperm can live in a woman's body for almost three days...."

"Cabe!" she gasped.

"My best friend studied to be a doctor," he said, unperturbed. "He told me a lot of things about women. The risk isn't just those few days, either, because some women ovulate irregularly, so you can't always be sure about when the dangerous time is. And stop blushing and looking at your feet. Reproduction is a natural, beautiful part of what a man and woman feel for each other. It's nothing to hide."

"A lot of people are making it into something to hide," she muttered. "And it isn't exactly loving these days, it's like...like blowing your nose, one girl said."

He drew her head against him. "Not for you and me, Dan," he said softly, using the nickname she was beginning to like. "You're no rounder, and I'm not into seducing virgins. It won't be something ugly and casual with us."

"It will if I'm just another conquest."

He kissed her forehead with breathless tenderness. "If you were going to be a conquest, I'd be adamant about birth control and something for both of us to use," he said at her temple. "Because these days only a fool takes chances in bed." He tilted her face up to his, and his eyes were quiet and solemn. "I don't care if you get pregnant, Dani. Does that sound casual?"

Her mind was whirling like a top. "I don't understand what you want," she faltered. "You said you didn't want commitment, and that you don't seduce virgins, and now you're talking about babies and..."

He smiled. "I like babies, Dani. Do you?"

"Oh, yes," she said, giving in to the madness. "I like to go in department stores and look at baby things," she confessed. Her shoulders rose and fell. "I never thought I'd have reason to buy any, but it was something to do when I was alone. I always seemed to be alone.''

"Me, too.'' He kissed her eyelids shut. ''I've been alone a long time. Then you came to work for me and started throwing calendars my way, and the light came back into the world. I didn't realize how I looked forward to each new day, until Christmas. I started to kiss you, and then I realized that you might think I was going to start chasing you and quit. And I knew that I couldn't make it without you at the office. There wouldn't be any joy left in the job.''

"I'd only just decided that it was you and not the job I went to work for,'' she confessed.

He sighed and brushed her mouth softly with his. "How can two people be so blind?'' he asked. "My dad was right, you know. You're worth two of Karol.''

She wanted to ask him about Karol, but she was afraid to. This might be just a slight infatuation on his part. She couldn't risk letting herself feel too much for him.

"The coffee,'' she said, glancing toward the pot.

"I guess we'd better do something about it before they send out a search party,'' he agreed with a sigh. "Okay. I'll slice the cake.'' He let her go and took a minute to tidy himself up while his cigarette smoldered and then finally went out in the ashtray. He sliced cake and Danetta put it onto saucers and got out forks and napkins to go with it, all neatly arranged on the big silver tray. Cabe picked it up and with one reluctant glance at Danetta, carried it into the living room.

Eight

Nicky was sent to bed at nine, and begged to have Norman sleep in his room. Cabe gave him a hard glare, but his parents agreed, providing it was all right with Danetta.

"You really let him run loose in your apartment?" Nicky asked excitedly when they'd brought Norman into the house and he was perched on a bookcase in Nicky's room.

"Yes, I really do. He's potty trained. We'll have to put down a slightly wet newspaper in your bathroom and show him where it is. He'll go straight to it."

"That's amazing," Nicky sighed. "Gosh, he's pretty."

"Don't talk too loud, you'll make him conceited," she said in a stage whisper.

Nicky laughed. "Okay."

"And for heaven's sake, don't leave your door open," she groaned. "He wanders at night. He isn't nocturnal, and he's supposed to stay put, but he can't read the book that says so."

"If he got into bed with my brother, the world would end, right?"

She had to stop and think a minute before she realized he meant Cabe. She could see her rugged boss trapped in a room with an iguana. She started laughing and couldn't stop.

"Are you sure that thing shouldn't be in a cage?" the object of their amusement asked from the doorway, scowling at Norman as he sprawled on the top of Nicky's bookcase.

"I'm absolutely sure," Danetta assured him. "He's very quiet and clean, and he won't bother anything. I was just telling Nicky how to fix his . . . toilet facilities."

"I could suggest a way," he murmured dryly.

"He's just a baby," Danetta said gently.

"Some baby. *Uggggggh*." Cabe shuddered.

"Close your ears, sweetheart," Danetta told the lizard, stroking his head gently. He closed his eyes instead, and Nicky laughed with pure delight.

"You made his day," Cabe said as he walked her to her own room on the other side of Nicky's. Cabe's was on the other side of the boy, so Danetta could understand his faint unease. In fact, they shared a mutual bathroom when Cabe was at home. She prayed that Nicky wouldn't forget to keep the doors closed.

"He's a nice boy," she replied, pausing with her hand on her doorknob. It was early to go to bed, but she was tired and hadn't had much sleep the night before. Besides, Cabe had mentioned something about going fishing early the next morning, even if it was dreary.

"I'll round you up a pole and we'll drive over to the lake and fish off Dad's pier," he murmured, his eyes going over her wan face like tender hands. "You look tired."

"It was a long night," she told him, "and I didn't get much sleep."

"That makes two of us," he mused, smiling faintly. "I tormented myself with thoughts of you and my sales manager until about five in the morning. I'd only had an hour's sleep when you got to the office."

She searched his pale blue eyes quietly. "Ben is a nice young man," she told him. "But I really went out with him to...well, to prove that I didn't have a crush on you. So you wouldn't think I was going to chase you, or anything."

He framed her face in his warm hands. "I might enjoy having you chase me, little one," he murmured. "You're something of a novelty in my life."

Which was just what she'd suspected all along. But he bent and kissed her gently, and she sighed with pure delight. Even knowing how shallow his feelings were didn't seem to do anything for her sense of self-preservation.

He lifted his head seconds later with obvious reluctance. "It isn't a good idea to start things we can't finish," he sighed. "Sleep tight, honey. Cynthia will drag you out of bed at daylight. She and Dad are early risers, and she cooks a big breakfast."

"I love breakfast," she said. "So does Norman. He likes eggs and bacon."

He shook his head. "Talk about your weird triangles," he murmured. "You and me and the Irish lizard. Good night."

She laughed as he walked away, her eyes adoring the powerful set of his shoulders, his slim waist and narrow hips and long legs. He was the most beautiful man she'd ever seen. All muscle and bristling masculinity and sensuous appeal. With a frustrated sigh, she went back into her room and closed the door.

The smell of bacon woke her long before Cynthia tapped on the door. She got up quickly, put on her jeans and a button-up blue-checked shirt and her socks and boots. It was still gray outside, but the sun was threatening to come

out and it had stopped raining. She ran a brush through her
hair, left off her makeup, brushed her teeth and rushed
down to breakfast.

Cabe was already in the kitchen taking platters of food
to the table for Cynthia. He looked different. His usual suit
had been sacrificed for tight jeans, a pair of boots that
made him even taller than usual and a pearl-snap Western-
cut chambray shirt. He looked the picture of a working
cowboy, and so sexy that he made Danetta's heart beat like
a drum.

She watched him while they ate, covertly she thought,
but Cynthia and Eugene were exchanging conspiratorial
glances, so maybe she was a bit more obvious than she'd
thought. In any event, Cabe was watching her openly, so it
didn't really matter.

Nicky was given the coveted chore of feeding Norman,
which he did with relish as they carried the lizard back out
to the garage for the daylight hours. And afterward, Cabe
rounded up his fishing gear and a pole for her and they
borrowed Eugene's fishing truck to drive to the lake.

Cabe looked perfectly at home in the truck, with a beat-
up tan Stetson on his dark hair. The sun was climbing out
from behind the clouds as they rode down the long dirt path
that led past an enormous barn where Eugene kept his
prize-winning purebred bulls. The path led into another
ranch road, which merged with a county paved road.

"I've walked it in the past," he chuckled. "There's a
shortcut, but it's still about two miles even that way. And
it's too long a hike with fishing gear and lunch." Lunch was
a big basket. Cynthia had packed it for them, along with
dessert and cold drinks, in a cooler in the back of the truck.
He glanced at her with a wry grin. "I don't relish the idea
of lugging coolers and baskets along, but Cynthia seemed
certain that we'd starve otherwise."

"Cynthia is nice," she replied. "And so is your half brother."

He averted his gaze to the road, accelerating to a speed that was distinctly uncomfortable for his passenger. "So everyone says."

She sighed wistfully. So much for mending broken fences, she thought.

They unloaded everything onto Eugene's wooden pier beside his boat house on the lake, along with the worms they'd stopped to dig behind the barn. Eugene kept his own bed of night crawlers there so he wouldn't have to hunt bait when he went fishing.

"Can you bait a hook all by yourself?" Cabe asked amusedly.

"Look, I grew up doing this," she informed him, deftly threading a worm on to her hook.

"Good God, that's not the way to do it," he burst out. "You have to give the fish something to nibble on!" He held up his own hook, where ten or so worms wiggled.

"You'll lose all your bait, and I'll get a fish," she said haughtily.

"You're on."

They threw their lines in and sat. In the distance, they heard motorboats, but Eugene's cabin and pier were in a small private cove, and no one intruded. Far out, the white triangle sails of the sailboats flashed against the blue sky.

The pier was weatherbeaten and wet, although the sun was beginning to dry it out nicely, but Cabe had produced plastic bags for them to sit on. It was quiet and somewhat magical to be here alone with him in the early morning, with no other human being around.

"I wish I had some dough-balls," she sighed. "We used to fish for crappie with them."

"Well, worms work pretty good on bass, unless you'd like to try spring lizards."

She gave him her best glare.

He shrugged. "Norman has cousins, I gather," he mused. He frowned in mock thoughtfulness. "I wonder what I'd catch if I put Norman on a hook...?"

"You'd catch hell, that's what you'd catch," she said. "Norman is not fish bait."

"I didn't sleep a wink for worrying about the doors staying closed," he muttered. "I figured if he's half as smart as you claim, he could open the damned door and eat me in my sleep."

She laid down her pole. "Now look here, for the last time, iguanas do not eat people. Especially not tough old oil riggers who probably taste like mildewed leather!"

He put down his own pole with a wicked grin, and the next thing she knew, she was flat on her back on the pier with him looming over her.

"I don't taste like mildewed leather, and I can prove it," he murmured, and lowered his hard, warm mouth square over hers.

She didn't even make a pretence of resisting. She reached up to hold him, drawing his weight down over her with soft resignation. He knew she wanted him, so there wasn't really much point in acting as if she didn't.

His mouth worked on hers in lazy little patterns, making her breath come quickly in her throat. His hands slid under her, protecting her back from the hardness of the pier while his face brushed hers and his lips and teeth nibbled sensually at her mouth.

"What do I taste like?" he whispered into her parted lips.

"Coffee," she whispered back. Her fingers touched his mouth, feeling the smooth skin above it where he'd shaved that morning, savoring the clean smell of his body. His eyes were pale and they narrowed as they searched hers. He looked down at her breasts where their faint cleft was visible in the deep V-neck of the button-up blue-checked shirt she was wearing.

"I'd give a lot to have you behind a locked door right now," he whispered huskily.

"What would you do?" she whispered.

"You know that already," he groaned against her mouth. His hand slipped around her rib cage to smooth over her soft breast with arrogant possession. "Remember how it felt, when I put my mouth on you?"

All too well. She moaned at the expert touch of his fingers on the taut rise of her breast, his thumb slowly driving her mad as it rubbed lazily against the small hardness.

He lifted his head, his dark face drawn as he looked around them. The area was totally deserted, and when his hungry eyes came back to hers, she knew before he reached for the buttons what he meant to do.

"Someone... might come looking for you," she whispered, but it was no real protest.

"If anyone does, I'll kill him," he said shortly. He had the blouse unbuttoned and out of her belted jeans. She was wearing a bra, and he groaned with pure impatience as he half lifted her, reaching around to unfasten it. "I hate these things," he muttered.

She stiffened as he moved to strip the blouse and bra away. "Cabe, you can't...!" she exclaimed.

"Yes, I can," he bit off, bending his head to her breasts.

The protests left, along with most of her breath and sanity as she felt the warm, moist pressure of his mouth taking the swollen tip inside. Her hands clenched beside her head and she moaned softly, arching faintly toward the sweet ferocity of his mouth.

His free hand moved to her nape, slid into her hair and held her, while the other made exciting little forays down to her belt and slowly under it, onto her flat belly.

She gasped, and he lifted his head to look into her shocked, apprehensive eyes.

"All right," he whispered when he saw the uncertainty in her face. He drew his hand out of her jeans and smoothed it up over her breasts. "We'll save that for a time when we can lock a door."

"I guess... what we're doing is pretty old hat to you," she said nervously.

His brows jerked together and then relaxed as he searched her eyes. "Dani," he began deeply, "it never felt like this with anyone else." The words came with obvious difficulty. He looked down at his hand, where it was gently stroking one firm, perfect breast and making her body tremble. "It was never this exciting to touch a woman intimately, to watch her reactions." His eyes went back to hers. "I'm capable right now," he whispered. "And I've barely touched you."

Capable had connotations, but she stared up at him blankly.

"You don't understand, do you?" he asked gently. Holding her eyes, he moved so that his forearms caught his weight. "Don't panic. I'm just going to show you something." Then he shifted, levering himself onto her body so that his hips and thighs pressed completely over hers.

Her eyes grew wide and shocked as she felt him intimately, and her lips parted.

"Capable," he whispered. His hands tangled in her hair and his eyes darkened and grew fiery with need as he bent toward her mouth. "Until this happens, a man isn't capable of intimacy with a woman, didn't you know...?"

His mouth covered hers and she shivered at the stark realization of what she was inviting. Age-old fears stiffened her, made her afraid.

"Shhhh," he breathed against her lips. "I'm not going to hurt you, little one. It's all right."

His slow, calm voice soothed her. Little by little, her body relaxed. His mouth warmed hers while he lifted just enough to get his shirt unbuttoned. Then he lowered his body again and she felt the springy hair on his chest rubbing abrasively against the delicate skin of her breasts.

A sound worked its way out of her mouth and into his, something that sounded alien and unfamiliar to her ears.

His mouth slid down to her ear. "You're shaking like a leaf," he breathed, nibbling the earlobe. His hand slid along her thigh, gently caressing. "Yes, you want me," he breathed. "And I want you."

She bit his shoulder through the thin fabric of his shirt and a sob muffled against it. "Cabe," she whispered achingly.

"Oh, God, I want you!" he groaned as his mouth worked its way back to hers. "I want a bed, and you in it, and the door locked and bolted . . ."

She opened her mouth for him, drowning in the sweet ardor that was making hellish demands on her untried body. She didn't understand the urge to bite, but he didn't seem to mind her teeth sliding against his broad shoulder, her lips on what she could reach of his broad, hairy chest. He even encouraged her, lifting himself so that she could reach the sensitive nipple on his own chest, her lips inexpert but fervent as she kissed him there.

He shuddered and groaned, grappling for her hand. He bent and kissed her hungrily, sliding her hand down his powerful body until it reached the core of his masculinity. He opened her fingers and pressed them against him. But her shocked struggle to draw her hand away brought him to his senses. He hadn't realized how far things had gone until then. And this just wasn't the place for what they were working toward. Damn circumstances! He didn't know how he was going to go on like this, with his conscience giving him hell every time he touched her and his body giving him hell every time he had to let her go. The situation was becoming impossible.

With a faint groan, he released her hand and rolled away from her. After a minute, he dragged himself into a sitting position. He was shivering faintly, and the hand that reached for his cigarettes trembled.

She sat up and got back into her things, curious to notice that he didn't even look her way. His back was razor straight and he was scowling. Maybe he was frustrated, she thought, a little embarrassed at her own headlong response.

His dark, wavy hair was mussed from her fingers, and his shirt was rumpled where it had been bunched to one side while they were making love. He looked sensuous and she sighed with lingering appreciation. At least he'd stopped before things got too much out of hand, but he looked different suddenly—withdrawn and brooding.

He drew in a steadying breath and smoked his cigarette in silence, not looking at her or saying a word to her until the silence became frankly uncomfortable. The fishing poles were still lying in their place, and Danetta stared at them blankly, wondering if anything had taken the bait.

Abstractedly he watched the sailboats far in the distance while he smoked his cigarette. "I'll be thirty-seven in a few months," he said. "Funny, I never thought about getting older. I was so busy building up my business and making money that time slipped away from me. I'm rich as hell, but I've got nothing. I go home to an empty apartment and an empty life. Until Christmas there was an occasional diversion. Since Christmas—" his eyes darkened as he looked at her "—there's been nothing at all." He lifted the cigarette to his lips and searched her quiet face. "Celibacy hasn't even been that difficult. I take Karol out and I can't touch her. She doesn't appeal to me because she isn't you. And I didn't even know it until a few days ago when I kissed her in my office and it was your mouth I tasted, your body I was imagining in my arms." He smiled at her faint surprise. "So now you know, don't you? I've been putting up a front for four months. Now the walls are down." The smile faded and his eyes began to narrow, to brighten with emotion. "I want you. By God, I do, and you want me. Except for your puritan morals and my conscience, we'd be lovers by now. It can't go on like this, Dan," he said finally. "We've got to decide what we're going to do."

So that was what was bothering him. He had a conscience and he couldn't bring himself to seduce her unless she was willing. But he didn't want commitment, either. Why should that surprise her, she wondered miserably, when he'd been saying it for two years? Her eyes lowered to the chest she'd stroked so hungrily, visible where his shirt was still unbuttoned. She hated being so vulnerable, and having him know it. She sighed as she drew up her knees and rested her chin on them to follow his gaze out over the lake. "Maybe it would be better for both of us if I go to work somewhere else," she said quietly, gritting her teeth in case he agreed with her. She didn't want to leave, but she wasn't cut out for an affair.

That wasn't the answer he'd expected. His head turned and he glared at her. She wanted him, he knew she did. He'd expected her to give in by now, but she was stubborn.

"Do you think leaving is going to solve anything?" he asked. He lifted the cigarette to his lips with a sharp, angry movement of his hand. "I want you, damn it!"

Her body stiffened. "Cabe, I'm not modern..." she began.

He saw the words in her mind and exploded with frustrated desire. Any other woman would have fallen into his arms. But this stubborn little virgin was going to deny herself and him, and for what? Well, if she was holding out for a wedding ring, he'd soon disabuse her of that fantasy. Just being around his father and Cynthia had distorted his perspective all over again. Love didn't last. If it did, his father could never have remarried!

"You're so damned bristly with hang-ups," he said harshly, glaring at her. "No sex before marriage, no allowances for human emotion. You're the ice maiden, all right. But we aren't living in the Dark Ages. It's permissible for a woman to sleep with a man she cares for. My God, Dani, don't you know what century this is?"

She felt her own temper letting go. She stood. "Yes, I know. And don't read me any lectures on the advantages of the modern world, either. Birth control was supposed to give women sexual freedom, but all I see it doing is giving men another excuse to stay single. Why marry anybody when you can sleep with whoever you please? And if you get pregnant, there are plenty of 'modern' alternatives to the problem . . . !"

That remark stung him. He stood, too, towering over her. "If you got pregnant by me, I'd stand by you. Besides, I'd be careful to protect you to start off with."

"Well, it could happen anyway," she shot back. "No birth control measure is absolute, not even the Pill. And men can afford to be careless, they can't get pregnant!"

His angry eyes shimmered like blue fires. "How did pregnancy get into this conversation?"

"It goes with sex," she returned with uncharacteristic sarcasm. His whole attitude infuriated her. "Didn't you know?"

He stood looking down at her with conflicting emotions. She looked different when she bristled. Her gray eyes lost their softness and began to take on the sheen of polished silver. Her exquisite complexion pinkened and glowed. Her body tautened, rippled with movement. He wanted to grab her and throw her down on the pier and have her...

His body betrayed him. Infuriated at it and at her, he turned away to button his shirt. "Well, don't expect any proposals of marriage from me," he said coldly, because she'd backed him into a corner and he felt trapped. "I want you, but not that much."

"Great, because marriage to a man like you is the last thing in the world I want!" she returned furiously. Later, when she remembered what he'd said, it would hurt like mad. But right now she was too upset to care.

"That delights me." He reached down and swung up his hat, slamming it on his head. "Get the poles, if you don't mind," he muttered as he picked up the cooler and the basket. "We can eat at home."

"That suits me fine." She picked up the poles. "In fact, I'm not hungry..." She noticed as she pulled the poles up that her line tightened. With a frown, she put his down and jerked on hers. On the end of the line was a big bass, wriggling furiously. "Well, what do you know," she exclaimed with a grin. "I caught a fish!" She glanced down at his own line. "Your worms are all gone," she said with mock sympathy. "Gee, that's too bad."

He glared at her. "It wasn't the worm that caught that bass," he said shortly. "He probably heard you expounding your archaic theories about sex and laughed himself to death."

"Why, you...!" She let fly with the bass, knocking his hat off and giving him a hard swipe on one lean cheek with the wet fish.

He took the fish string away from her with a curt jerk of his hand, angrily wiping his face on his sleeve before he picked up his hat and stuck it back on his head. "Hit me with a fish, will you?" he growled, glaring at her as he moved forward.

She backed up. "You deserved it," she said. Her lower lip was trembling and unshed tears glistened in her eyes. "You philanderer!"

The tears slowed him down, but only physically. "That's better than being an icy little prude," he returned.

She turned away, shakily, and picked up the fishing poles. He didn't even spare her a glance. He was shocked at her behavior and even more shocked at his own. Things had been developing so sweetly between them, and all of a sudden they were enemies. He didn't even realize how it had happened. He'd wanted her so badly, but he couldn't give her what she wanted in return. He wasn't going to marry her just for the brief pleasure her body could give him. If only she hadn't started talking about getting pregnant. He almost groaned out loud at the thought of somebody else's child in her body. It would happen one day, because she was pretty and sweet and other men would want her. Ben already did. He felt sick at the memory of Ben looking at her. With a furious curse, he turned and stomped off toward the pickup, leaving her to follow or not.

It was the first real argument they'd ever had, unless she counted the day she'd told him what she thought of him. He was fuming, and it showed even in the way he drove the truck back to Eugene's ranch.

"I'd better go back to my apartment," she said stiffly.

"No, ma'am," he returned curtly as he parked the truck. "The whole idea of having you here was for your own protection until I could have a private detective go over your place and find out who broke into it, and why. Dad and I have been working on that since late yesterday. He had a call in to your cousin Jenny first thing this morning, as well." He turned to glare at her. "You'll stay until tomorrow at least." He smiled, but it was more a cold twist of his lips. "I'm sure I can trust you not to attack in my sleep."

She glared at him coldly and got out of the truck.

For the rest of the day, she ignored him. She helped Cynthia in the kitchen by scaling and filleting the bass while Eugene and Cabe locked themselves in the study with business. Later Cabe went out to the garage where Nicky was feeding his own pets and Norman. His mind was in revolt and his body still ached for the taste of Danetta he'd had that morning.

Nicky looked up as his half brother came into the game room, a pretty male anole on his hand.

"I thought you and Dani had gone fishing," he remarked to the older man, still a little shy with him.

Cabe shrugged, smoking his cigarette quietly. "She caught a bass. I guess it will be on the supper menu. What's that thing?"

"It's an anole," Nicky told him. "Anolis Carolinensis. They're called 'new world chameleons.' They change color and they're very tame. Want to hold him?"

Cabe shuddered. "I'm not a lizard lover."

"Technically, I guess they are reptiles," Nicky replied as he returned the tiny thing to its cage. "Doesn't he look just like a miniature crocodile?" he mused. "But Norman is the neatest guy..."

Norman had spotted Cabe from the high wire wall of his temporary home. He bristled immediately, dropping his dewlap as he got down from the wall, and twisted his body into an imitation of a cat's attack pose and lifted his elegant tail over his head.

"Hi, pal," Cabe told the big lizard. "I love you, too."

"He's afraid of you," Nicky explained. "They aren't aggressive at all except during mating season. Then they get real bad tempered."

"I can understand that," Cabe said under his breath.

"He's just nervous and you're awful big," Nicky continued. He made a production of wiping off the cage. "I like Dani," he added hesitantly. "Are you going to marry her?"

Cabe's face closed up. "Hell, no!"

"Oh."

"She's my secretary," he added when he saw the wounded look on the boy's face at his curt tone.

"She knows a lot about lizards," Nicky remarked. "Most girls are scared of them. Mom is, although she hides it pretty good."

Cabe sat down on the plush sofa nearby, across from the billiard table, and crossed his long legs. He pulled an ash-tray close on the coffee table. "How's school?" he asked.

"Great," Nicky replied with a smile. "I got to go to the Will Rogers museum on a field trip this month. He was a neat guy."

"So he was." He studied the boy quietly, thinking that someday if he ever married, he might have a son of his own. "What are you going to be when you grow up?"

"A zoologist," Nicky said without hesitation. "I'm going to take a lot of biology courses later on, and zoology when I get to college. I want to specialize in herpetology."

"Well, this should be good practice for you," he nodded toward the anoles and gekkos and frogs in their neat aquariums. "You'd do a good job of keeping those habitats true to life, and clean."

Nicky beamed. "Thanks, Cabe."

He lifted his cigarette to his lips. "Has Dad taught you much about the oil business? Even if you won't take an active part in it, it doesn't hurt to know something about how it works."

Nicky moved closer, his hands behind him. "Dad stays busy," he replied.

That had been the story of Cabe's young life. His father was forever away at some new oil field or offshore rig. He'd traveled all over the world, and Cabe and his mother had been left alone a good deal of the time. Funny, he'd expected that Eugene would settle when he remarried. He seemed to care about Cynthia a lot. But as Cabe pondered the situation, he realized that most of Eugene's regard toward Nicky was monetary in nature. He gave the boy anything he wanted—except attention and time.

"Haven't you ever seen a rig operating?" Cabe persisted.

Nicky shook his head.

Cabe studied his cigarette. "One of my customers has a big rig down around Beggs," he said hesitantly. He looked up to catch a strangely hopeful look on the boy's face. "I could take you down there next weekend." He smiled. "I used to work as a rigger."

"I know. Dad told me. Would you really, Cabe?" he asked shyly. "I'd really like that. If I wouldn't be too much trouble. Dad says I'm a wild one."

Wild for attention, probably. Cabe got up and ruffled the boy's hair affectionately. "You won't be any trouble, sprout," he said gently, grinning at Nicky's rapt stare. "Let's go see if we can find something to do besides look at lizards." He glared back at Norman. "Don't they eat iguanas in Latin America?" he asked hesitantly.

"Yes, they do," Nicky said. "They call them *gallina de palo*—chicken of the tree. They're supposed to taste like chicken. But you can't!" he exclaimed. "Dani would never forgive you!"

Cabe sighed as they walked out the door. "I have a feeling she won't, in any case," he said bleakly when he remembered the things he'd said to her out of frustration. He could have been gentler, he thought miserably. He didn't like remembering the tears in her eyes. He didn't like it at all.

Nine

———

Danetta didn't look at Cabe during lunch, or speak to him. Fortunately Nicky was wound up about going to see the oil rig with Cabe the following weekend, and talked nonstop. Cynthia looked radiant when she saw the budding warmth of Cabe's relationship with Nicky. Even Eugene smiled. Danetta was glad about that, but Cabe had hurt her badly, and knowing what he really felt was killing her. She was only a body to him after all, only a prospective affair. He'd said before that he didn't want an affair, but it had probably been a red herring, to keep her from realizing too soon that he had nothing to offer except sex.

They ate the bass. It was fried and delicious, but Danetta hardly tasted it. She'd had such hopes for today. Now she knew that she'd never have anything else with Cabe.

"I fed Norman for you, Dani," Nicky told her. "Cabe thought he was going to eat him!" he added with a chuckle.

"He sure doesn't like you, does he?" he asked his half brother.

"I don't know," Danetta said, speaking for the first time. "With tenderizer and a little catsup, he might not taste half bad to Norman."

Everybody laughed. Even Cabe, but he noticed that she wouldn't meet his eyes.

"He's a vegetarian. You said so," he reminded her.

His tone was faintly conciliatory, but she wouldn't trust it. "I guess I did."

"Did you know that they're experimenting with cloning animal and vegetable matter together?" Nicky asked. "I read about it in a magazine. Imagine a carrot that had rabbit cells..."

Danetta only half heard him as she worked her way through lunch. She wanted to go home. Even the intruder didn't bother her half as much as being in the same house with Cabe after what he'd said to her.

"I've got this great new computer game, Cabe," Nicky mentioned as they were eating cake for dessert. "It's a mystery with cases to solve, and real good graphics. Dad said you used to like watching Sherlock Holmes movies, so I thought you might enjoy the game."

Cabe smiled at him gently. "Is that why you bought it?"

Nicky cleared his throat and blushed. "Well, sort of."

"I'd like to see it, Nicky," he replied, not regretting the impulsive decision for one instant when Nicky's face looked like Christmas had come. He glanced at Danetta, but her eyes were on her cake. She didn't look up, even when he left.

"World War III, hmmm?" Eugene asked, pursing his lips as he and Cynthia stared at Danetta.

"I beg your pardon?" she asked nervously.

"Cabe wants her, but without a wedding ring," Cynthia murmured dryly, nodding at Danetta's shocked expression. "We know him very well," she added gently. "You stick to your guns. He's never brought anybody home to us before, and you're unique. He'll give in. You'll see."

"All you have to do is play him a little," Eugene instructed, leaning forward. "You know, like a big, stubborn fish. Give him enough line and he'll hook himself."

"It's not that simple...." she faltered.

"Sure it is," he replied. "He's halfway there already, or why would he have brought you home?"

"But I told you," she moaned. "My apartment was broken into."

"He could have sent you to a hotel, honey," Cynthia said, patting her hand gently. "Or let you come down here alone." She shook her pretty blond head. "No, he didn't have to come with you at all."

Eugene chuckled as he sipped black coffee. "Even worse, he's been roaring around like a mad bull trying to find out who burgled you. Made him furious that you were threatened."

She took all this with a grain of salt, but it made her feel a little better.

"Have you heard from Jenny?" she asked.

He nodded. "And our private detective checked in just before you and Cabe came back from the lake. We've got something planned. Jenny's flying in tomorrow, and you can go home tomorrow night. Cabe will explain it to you."

She didn't think so. He didn't seem enthusiastic about even spending five minutes with her for the rest of the day. He played the computer game with Nicky and talked to his father, and generally relaxed. Danetta helped Cynthia dig in her newly planted flower garden in the yard, enjoying the manual labor as she hadn't enjoyed anything for a long time. Then they started supper. Before Danetta knew it, bedtime was looming and Cabe still hadn't told her anything about their plan.

He talked to Eugene about it, though, absently, with his eyes out the window instead of on the subject at hand.

"You're preoccupied," Eugene said bluntly. "It's Danetta, isn't it?"

It was unusual to talk about personal things with his father. He realized with a start that he never had. He turned. "Yes. It's Danetta. We've reached an impasse. I want her, but she wants commitment." He stuck his hands into his pockets and moved restlessly closer to the picture window, staring out at Eugene's cattle. "I don't trust emotions very much. They don't last."

"Don't they?" Eugene perched on the corner of his desk. "I guess you got that idea from me because I married Cynthia instead of going on with just the memory of your mother."

Cabe turned, his blue eyes faintly accusing. "That's about the size of it."

Eugene smiled wistfully. "Your mother and I were married when she was eighteen and I was twenty-two because her parents and my parents thought it would be a good idea. I had a career and some small amount of fame and a good deal of money. They had nothing. I didn't want commitment, either, but your mother did." He shook his head. "We got married in a fever and it didn't burn out in thirty years, boy," he said huskily, and there was something in his eyes that stopped Cabe in his tracks. "I married Cynthia because it was that or kill myself. That's how much I missed your mother. I'll tell you the truth, if you want it," he added with cold anger. "I tried to blow my brains out. Cynthia happened to come over to get some papers to sign—she was my secretary in case you've forgotten—and she took the pistol away and seduced me."

"My God." Cabe sat down on the sofa, heavily.

"So now you know it all, don't you, boy?" Eugene asked. "There was every chance that I'd made Cynthia pregnant in the fever of it, and I couldn't very well die and leave her alone with my child. We got married in a real rush, and Nicky came along nine months later to the day." He smiled at Cabe's shocked expression. "Does that answer all the questions you've avoided asking me for eight years?"

"I'm sorry," Cabe said with quiet sincerity. "I'm sorry I didn't talk to you about it before. Long before. I don't like remembering the way I've treated Cynthia and Nicky. I won't get over it easily."

"Cynthia understood," he replied. "She didn't want me to tell you, in fact." He chuckled mirthlessly. "She thought it might lessen me in your eyes to find out that I'd been even briefly suicidal."

"On the contrary," Cabe returned. "It would have turned my life around. We all owe Cynthia a lot."

"Not the least of all for Nicky," Eugene said quietly. "It was like having you back, all over again. Except that I seem to be making the same mistake with him. Keeping him in a corner and going overboard at work." He sighed. "I should have taken him to see those oil rigs myself. You knew that, didn't you?"

Cabe grinned. "No problem. You can come with us, if you like."

Eugene lifted a thick silvery eyebrow. "There's a suggestion. Why not? Both my boys with me on an outing. I guess I can take it if you can."

"You're all right," Cabe said with gruff affection.

"So are you," Eugene said, equally gruff. He cleared his throat. "What are you going to do about Danetta?"

Cabe sighed. "I don't know."

"She's a proud woman. If you don't watch it, she'll walk out. You'll never find another one like her."

"I know that." He raked his hand through his hair. "It's the idea of marriage. Of being tied."

"We all come to it, boy," Eugene said quietly. "Marriage is what you make of it. Your mother and I were happy. Cynthia and I have been, too." He smiled at his son. "There are a hell of a lot of compensations."

"Like sex?" Cabe asked mockingly.

"Someone to come home to," Eugene added. "Someone to sit up with you when you're sick. Someone to talk to when the world closes in. A willing pair of hands when you want help. A loving voice when you hurt." He smiled reminiscently. "Sex, sure, that's a healthy, good part of marriage. But without being involved emotionally, it's like scratching your back when it itches. Feels good at the time, but ten minutes later, you don't remember doing it."

Cabe chuckled softly. "God, what an analogy!"

"Danetta's a virgin, isn't she?" Eugene asked with his usual bluntness.

Cabe actually blushed. "Now see here . . . !" he began, outraged.

Eugene got up and patted his son on the shoulder with rough affection. "Take a long time with her. It will be all right. And get married, son. Virgins these days are like diamonds on Main Street. Rare."

He walked out, leaving a poleaxed, ruddy-complexioned Cabe staring blindly in front of him. All those years of blaming his father for his infidelity to his mother's memory, only to learn a staggering truth. So love did last. Cynthia must have loved Eugene a great deal to make the sacrifice she had, to risk everything for him, even getting pregnant with his child to hold him to life. He frowned thoughtfully. Did Danetta have that depth of feeling for him? All at once he was almost convinced that he had it for her. He had to know if it was returned, if she cared enough to make an equal commitment to him. The future loomed dark and uninviting before him when he thought that she was going to be looking for another job come Monday.

Meanwhile Danetta was trying to find out about the plan for returning her to her apartment, and getting nowhere. Cabe came out of Eugene's office looking oddly thoughtful and remote, except that his brooding stare kept homing to her until her nerves were standing up screaming. He didn't want her, he'd said so, not in any emotional way. So why was he staring at her like that?

"About Jenny..." she began as the television was turned off at eleven.

"Tomorrow," Cabe said quietly. His pale eyes searched hers for a long, electric moment, but she was through playing games. She turned away. Nicky had gone to bed an hour earlier with Norman cradled in his arms. Norman had warmed to the boy quickly, and seemed to actually enjoy being carried around by him. Danetta thought that it was probably going to be hard for Nicky to say goodbye to the big lizard.

She said her good-nights and went into her room, closing the door quietly. Monday she was going to start looking in the want ads for another job, she decided bitterly. She'd had all she could stand of her blow-hot-blow-cold boss, and she wasn't having any affairs with him. Her eyes narrowed as she got into her pale lemon-yellow, see-through gown. It had been an impulse purchase, because she'd fallen in love with the lacy low-cut garment the minute she saw it. Not that anyone would ever see her in it, she sighed, looking at her slender, sexy body in the mirror. But it did look sharp on her. She laid her matching robe over a chair and climbed into bed.

It took forever for her to get to sleep. She'd tried not to think about what had happened earlier, although it still stung. But she'd only been asleep for a few minutes when a shout woke her.

She heard it in the back of her mind and sat straight up. Maybe she was imagining things, she thought as she listened.

"Help!"

No, there it was again, and unless she was going deaf, it was Cabe.

She put on her robe and went sleepily down the hall to his room. His door was open a crack and she could hear voices across the hall as she walked into Cabe's bedroom and stopped dead.

There was a small bedside lamp burning. Norman was at the foot of Cabe's bed in his attack position, with his dewlap down and his tail raised, looking ferocious—like a miniature iguanodon. Cabe, without a stitch of clothing on, was standing on the bed near the headboard, backed against the wall, brandishing a lamp that was companion to the one on the other side of the bed.

Danetta's shocked eyes lingered on his muscular, hairroughened body for a staggering minute. She'd never seen a real live nude man in her life, and Cabe was just devastating. He was all man, and so sensuous that she had to drag her eyes away from him. Darkly tanned skin, even where swimming trunks would have been, long muscular legs, flat stomach...

"Norman!" she chided with her hands on her hips, forcing her eyes to stay on her pet.

The lizard didn't move. She sighed. Well, immediate action was called for. "Now Norman," she said quietly. She approached slowly and began to pet him, talking softly as she slid a hand under his body and lifted him gently. He whipped his tail, but after a minute, his dewlap began to go down and he relaxed, looking faintly bored instead of viciously homicidal.

Cabe had moved off the bed and found a robe, whipping it around his nude body.

"He's all right now," she assured him, glancing hesitantly his way to make sure he was covered.

"*He's* all right," he muttered, glaring at the reptile. "My God, I thought my number was up! I felt something cold and clammy against my foot and—"

"Clammy?" she gasped. "Norman is not clammy...!"

"—when I turned on the light, there was the Irish lizard practicing for the Darth Vader award!"

"He's just a baby, he wouldn't have hurt you," she defended.

"Like fun he wouldn't!" He righted the lamp that he'd laid on the bedside table.

"You weren't going to hit him with the lamp!" she exclaimed.

"No, I was going to throw it at him," he corrected darkly.

"Oh, shame on you!" she accused. "Why didn't you just get a newspaper and shoo him out?"

"Because I couldn't be sure that he wouldn't eat the newspaper for supper and me for dessert!"

"He doesn't eat people!"

"How do you know? Have you counted your relatives and neighbors lately?"

Eugene and Cynthia eased inside the room, looking from the lizard in Danetta's hands to Cabe's outraged expression.

"He escaped?" Eugene mused.

"Yes, he escaped, right out of Nicky's bedroom and into mine!" Cabe thundered. "He tried to climb me!"

"Weren't you nervous?" Cynthia exclaimed.

Cabe shifted. "A little," he admitted.

"He was standing in the middle of the bed yelling his head off," Danetta muttered.

"I was not!" Cabe shouted. "I was trying to get in the best position to heave the lamp at him!"

"How barbaric," Eugene murmured. "Poor Norman."

"He can't stay in the house," Cabe said doggedly. "I won't sleep next door to that creature."

"I'll put him out in the garage," Danetta said. "Is Nicky asleep?"

"Snoring," Cynthia said gently. "He never wakes up at night. He won't miss Norman."

"Will he be warm enough out there?" Eugene asked, frowning. "Suppose you close the game-room door and shut it off from the garage?" he suggested. "You can turn up the thermostat and he'll stay toasty warm."

"If you wouldn't mind," Danetta replied.

"Not at all. Cabe can show you how the door works," he added. "It's tricky."

"Could you . . . ?" Danetta began.

"I'm not afraid of the damned lizard," Cabe said defensively. "Come on."

She shrugged and went down the hall with Cabe. Cynthia and Eugene went back into their bedroom chuckling and closed the door.

"They'll laugh for weeks," Cabe muttered. He glared at Danetta. "You and your attack lizard."

"He isn't an attack lizard." She followed him into the garage. It was cold outside, but once they were in the game room and he shut it off from the garage, the chill was less noticeable.

Danetta put Norman gently in the cage and closed it, rubbing her arms. The robe wasn't much thicker than her gown, and she was cold.

Cabe had turned up the thermostat and switched on a small light. He was watching her, his pale eyes intent on the soft curves of her body through the thin fabric.

"You needn't get any ideas," she said shortly. "I didn't wear this gown for your benefit."

"I wish you had," he said with a heavy sigh. "It would mean you weren't still hurt by what I said to you this morning."

"What do you care if I was hurt?" she asked, turning away. "You don't want me except in bed."

He stuck his hands into the pockets of his dark robe. "That's what I said, wasn't it?" he asked bitterly.

He sat down on the comfortable sofa and pulled a cigarette from his pocket to light.

"Yes," she replied, ducking her head. "And I've decided that you're right. The best thing is for me to get another job. I can start looking Monday morning—"

"No!" he ground out. "Not yet."

She glanced at him nervously. "Why not? The sooner I go, the better!"

He blew out a thick cloud of smoke impatiently. He'd started this mess, now he had to find some way to calm things back down until he could decide how to handle it. "Not yet," he repeated doggedly. "Give it a couple of weeks. We've got to sort out your burglar first."

"Oh. I'd forgotten about him," she said, willing to use any excuse not to have to leave him. It was going to tear her heart out. He probably wouldn't even miss her.

With a long sigh she sat down at the other end of the sofa. "Eugene said you had something planned, and that Jenny is coming home tomorrow."

He took another draw from the cigarette and abruptly crushed it out. The action caused his robe to open in front, giving Danetta a much-too-revealing look at his chest and stomach. She averted her eyes, shaking all over with the need to be held and loved by him. The longing was so strong that she was amazed he couldn't see it, but he wasn't looking at her. "We're going to stake out your apartment. I'll explain it to you when Jenny gets there. It's rather complicated, but it should solve your problems."

She nodded. Her biggest problem was sitting two feet away, but she knew he wasn't going to offer any quick solutions to that one. "You and your brother seem to be getting along better," she said to break the tense silence.

"Yes, we are. He's a fine boy. I was thinking this afternoon that it wouldn't be unpleasant at all to have a son of my own." He glanced at her. "How do you feel about children?"

She shifted. "I like them." She twisted the skirt of her gown and robe nervously. "How are you going to have children when you don't want to get married?"

"I guess I'd have to get married." His pale eyes lanced over her, kindling as he noticed the way the soft yellow fabric clung to her exquisite body."

She swallowed. "To Karol?"

"Can you see Karol risking her figure to give me a child?"

She smiled faintly. "If she loved you, yes."

"Then you think a woman would want the risk if she loved a man?" he persisted quietly.

She nodded.

He lifted his head, staring at her with eyes that faintly smoldered. "Then why don't you come over here and let me put your body under mine on this sofa, and we'll make love."

Her eyes almost popped as they sought his, and she went scarlet. "I don't think I heard you . . ."

"Yes, you did," he said quietly. "You just got through saying that you like babies. So do I. Let's make one."

She got to her feet, shaking all over with reaction. "You're out of your mind. . . . You don't want commitment, you said so, you don't want . . . Cabe!"

He'd reached out during her rambling speech and caught her behind the legs. She tumbled into his arms and he eased her down beside him. In the struggle, his robe had opened even more, and she got the same eyeful she'd had in his bedroom. It knocked the breath right out of her, and she couldn't seem to drag her eyes away from his deeply tanned, hair-roughened muscles.

"This is superfluous," he said quietly, shouldering out of the robe. "You know what I look like by now."

"This is crazy," she whispered as she fought to hold on to her sanity.

"Not if you love me, Dani," he said, his voice deep and solemn. "If you do, and it's more than just an infatuation, I'm going to ease you out of your gown and robe and we're going to have each other right here. I don't know of any better way to convince you that I'm not afraid of commitment than by getting you pregnant deliberately."

"What will your father and stepmother say?" she exclaimed in desperation.

"Oh, that's a dandy little story. Remind me to tell you all about it one day." His hands were on her robe. "Tell me. Yes or no."

She trembled at his touch, her eyes like saucers. She hadn't counted on this, hadn't thought that it might happen.

"I'm scared," she confessed in a tiny whisper.

"So am I," he replied unexpectedly. "I suppose it's natural when two people make this kind of commitment to each other. You do understand that I'm talking about marriage, not living together? In that respect, I'm pretty old-fashioned myself."

"You might regret it later," she faltered. "It might be just a physical thing, the novelty of my innocence."

"Let's find out." He began to remove her robe and gown, hesitating for an instant to make sure she wanted it. But she didn't protest. He eased the fabric away from her body, catching his breath when all the creamy pink and white contours were revealed to his fascinated eyes. He lay just looking at her for a long time, not even touching her.

"You're blushing," he whispered when he was finally able to look into her eyes.

"I've never done this," she said with a painful smile. "It's more difficult than I thought not to grab for something to cover myself with."

"Why?" he asked gently. "You're exquisite. Like a delicate oil painting, in a very private gallery, for my eyes only." He brushed his hand over her shoulder lightly, feeling her tremble. "But a painting that I can touch. Here. And here."

His fingers drew over her breasts with slow, painfully sweet expertise, down to her flat stomach, her hips, her long legs. He kissed her in a way he never had, with such breathless tenderness that she relaxed completely.

"You're going to have to trust me completely, you understand that, don't you?" he whispered at her lips. "Because this is going to involve a kind of touching that you've never experienced, an intimacy that may shock you sometimes. Can you lie still under my hands and give me that freedom without fighting me and yourself?"

"I . . . think so," she whispered back. Her eyes searched his. She was already trembling from the sweetness of his touch, but even as she looked up at him, his hand moved down her body, and he held her gaze while he began to discover her in a frightening way.

He kissed her tenderly, tasting the soft gasp that escaped her throat. "I won't hurt you," he said tenderly. "I won't have to." He smiled against her lips when she tautened and shivered. "I hope you don't mind having the lights on, little one," he said as he deepened the kiss, "because I want to watch you."

Those were the last words that registered in her mind for a long time. He played her like a divine instrument, with his hands and his mouth, his tongue, even his teeth, while her heartbeat grew as loud and heavy as his, her faint trembling echoed in his powerful body as he guided her hands and aroused her body to a really frightening pitch.

He was lying beside her, not over her, and that position didn't change even when his hand slid to her hips and brought them into his with firm purpose.

"Open your eyes," he whispered, seeking and finding her drowsy gaze as he slid one long leg gently between hers and pulled her to him with incredible intimacy. She stiffened and he moved. "Steady, now," he whispered. "Let go. Don't be afraid, it's only going to hurt for a second." He moved again. She cried out softly, but her body accepted his almost at once, and his hand enforced the total possession of his body as he brought her hips to settle completely against his.

She shivered. "It's . . . so intimate," she whispered, still looking at his face. "Is . . . is it over?" she asked, because she didn't know.

He smiled, and shook his head, indulgent even as his own body went rigid and shuddered with its terrible need. "It's only beginning," he whispered, and his mouth covered hers.

There was a rhythm. It shocked her with its incredible pleasure, because every time he moved, terribly sweet sensations knifed through her taut stomach and up her spine. She bit his shoulder, his chest, her hands smoothing down his hairy chest and loving the way his legs rippled when she did. She could feel every beat of his heart, every rough sigh of his breath, every movement he made.

He was holding back, she knew, for her sake, and it touched her even more deeply. She began to move against him, trying to echo his own soft rhythm, feeling it slow and deepen as the first staggering tension racked her and dragged a high-pitched cry out of her throat.

"Soon," he ground out at her ear. "Soon, soon, soon...!" He groaned harshly and she felt his teeth against her upper arm. "God, I can't . . . get close . . . enough . . . !"

But he did, because the world around them dissolved in a molten red furor of movement and sound. She felt her body become rigid just seconds before his, and the tension broke in a staggering rush of heated pleasure that left her weeping in his powerful arms.

He felt her tears against his neck and was too totally exhausted to even kiss them away. He held her closer while he tried to breathe. A long time later, his lips touched her face with delicate wonder while he tried to cope with the most exquisite pleasure he'd ever known.

She started to pull back, but his hands caught her hips and held them against his.

He lifted his head, his sweaty dark hair curling onto his forehead as he met her shy, embarrassed eyes. "Don't pull away yet," he whispered roughly. "I'll die if you unlock your body from mine."

He sounded serious and she subsided, her eyes staring into his as she lay back down, red faced and trembling.

"You love me," he said gruffly. "No way on earth you would have let me do that if you didn't."

She swallowed. "It might have been an uncontrollable urge."

"But it wasn't." He drew his chest back just enough so that he could look down the length of their bodies, his eyes smoldering and intent, his jaw clenched. "My God, look . . . !"

She couldn't. Her face buried itself hotly in his throat.

"Don't be embarrassed," he whispered achingly. "Sweetheart, don't be, it's so beautiful."

She trembled at the emotion in his deep voice. "You've done it before," she whimpered.

"No!" He kissed her eyes shut. "Not like this, not ever. This is reverent," he breathed. "Creation. Rebirth." His arms contracted hungrily. "I want this again, endlessly, for the rest of my life."

Her breath caught in her throat as the words got through to her. It sounded as if he was telling her he loved her. Was he?

She drew her head away from his throat and looked into his pale blue eyes, her own uncertain, hesitant.

He brushed back her damp, curly hair with hands that shook slightly. "Did I satisfy you?" he asked huskily.

She hid her face again, shivering.

"Because if I didn't," he whispered shakily, his hands moving her in an impossibly sensuous arc against him, "I can now."

She shuddered, because she could feel that. Her hands gripped him. She wanted to say no, to ask him to tell her what he felt, but his mouth was on hers and he was shifting her gently onto her back, his body still joined to hers, and it was happening all over again. He shuddered uncontrollably as he made love to her, his voice shaking as he took her into realms they hadn't discovered before. At the last, his voice broke as he lifted her up to him and fulfilled her with a tenderness that she knew she'd never forget for as long as she lived.

When he finally moved away from her, he was pale and utterly exhausted, his face harder than she'd ever seen it.

He got up and reached for his robe, slipping into it without looking at her. He couldn't. She probably didn't realize that he'd just given her his soul. But he did, and he was scared to death. She owned him now. He'd do anything for her.

She got back into her own things, feeling a little ashamed and nervous. "Are you . . . are you all right?" she asked hesitantly.

"That's my line, isn't it?" He was smoking a cigarette. He turned, and looked down at her, his eyes quiet and intent on her wan face. "Yes, I'm all right. If you can call being shaken to the core of my soul being all right. Are you?"

She nodded, lowering her eyes to the floor. Her body tingled with new knowledge, with the faint soreness his hunger had expressed physically. She pleated her gown. "Are you sorry?" she whispered.

He wasn't sure if he was or not. He was too shaken to talk about it. He hadn't realized that he was capable of so much emotion, of such a deep, aching hunger for only one woman. "I don't suppose so," he said noncommittally. He took a long draw from the cigarette, unaware of the faint panic on Danetta's face because of his remoteness. "We'd better go inside."

She started toward the door. What had begun as sweet and sensual and earthshaking had turned into cold, stark reality. She'd just given herself to a man who was a self-professed bachelor. A man who didn't really believe in marriage or commitment, despite his uncontrollable hunger for her minutes before. He'd satisfied his hunger, now he was probably regretting the whole thing. He knew that she didn't sleep around. Probably he hadn't meant a word he'd said to her, because he'd been too aroused to think. She wanted to die. She was so ashamed of herself, and what in the world would she do if she got pregnant? Her carelessness was going to give her hell.

She went out the door ahead of him, her eyes downcast, her face pale and miserable. She didn't look at him, not once.

He hadn't noticed the effect his coolness was having on her. He was too shaken by his own discoveries to notice much at all. He smoked his cigarette in silence all the way to the house without saying a word.

It was only when they got to the door of the room Danetta was staying in that he saw the tears rolling down her cheeks.

"Here, now," he exclaimed softly, catching her arm.

She shook off his hand. "Good night," she said on a broken sob. She slammed into her room, catching him off guard, and locked it.

He stood there feeling like ten kinds of a fool. "Oh, my God," he breathed huskily. "Danetta!"

But she didn't answer him, not even when he tapped on the door. With a heavy sigh, he went back to his own room and closed the door. He'd been so wrapped up in his own shock that he hadn't realized how cold he must have seemed to her. She'd given him her chastity, and he'd taken it without a single word afterward about how he felt or how committed he was. She was crying and it was his fault.

The look on her face would haunt him until morning. He only hoped he could straighten things out in time. It was bad enough that she was going to spend the night hating herself and him for what she'd be sure to think was premeditated seduction. Especially after the hurtful things he'd said to her on the pier.

He tossed and turned miserably. His conscience was killing him. Of course he wanted commitment! After an experience like that, only an idiot wouldn't realize that love was at the bottom of it.

Finally he closed his eyes and forced himself not to worry about the damage he'd done. He'd talk to her in the morning. Somehow he'd make her understand how he felt.

He got up earlier than usual and rushed downstairs, still tucking his blue chambray shirt into his jeans, when he noticed that Eugene and Cynthia and Nicky were at the table and Danetta wasn't.

"Where's Danetta?" Cabe asked curtly.

Eugene grimaced. "Well, son, she came downstairs all packed and ready to go, picked up Norman and got a cab back to Tulsa before any of us were up. She left this note."

He handed it to Cabe. It was brief and to the point. *Had to go home. Thanks for your hospitality. Danetta Marist.*

Cabe sat down heavily at the table. He'd sure fouled everything up now!

Ten

Danetta rode back to Tulsa in a daze, trying not to think about what the fare was going to be. She'd already asked the driver if he'd take a check, and because she looked so distraught and miserable, the driver had broken a lifelong rule and agreed. Thank God she had her checkbook with her.

She didn't want to think about what had happened to her in the garage with Cabe. A lifetime of honorable living, and she'd blown it all in one night because she'd let her body dictate to her mind. She cringed trying to imagine how she was going to tell her parents if she became pregnant.

She wondered how Cabe was feeling, and decided that her impulsive action had probably saved him a lot of embarrassment. He'd shown last night how he regretted what he'd done, even if he hadn't cared enough to at least apologize for it. Probably he thought she'd gotten what she deserved for letting him go that far, and she couldn't put all the blame on him. She could have said no.

The cab pulled up at her apartment building. She wrote him a check, smiling wanly as she thanked him and handed it to him. He carried her suitcase and Norman's carrying case to the door for her, a kindness that had her in tears. He even looked reluctant to leave her there, although he hadn't been reluctant to leave the iguana. Creepy kind of pet, he thought as he went back to the elevator. But a real nice young lady.

She unlocked the door and walked in, and came face-to-face with Cousin Jenny.

"Surprise, it's me!" Jenny grinned, and then stopped dead at Danetta's expression. "Why, honey, what's wrong?" she asked in a gentler tone.

Danetta put Norman and the suitcase down and closed the door before she collapsed against the wall in tears.

Jenny hugged her, without asking questions, and then made her sit down in the kitchen while she made coffee.

"Norman..." Danetta began brokenly, wiping at tears with a hem of her blouse.

"I'll let him out," Jenny said, swallowing hard. She flipped the catch and opened the door, quickly standing back.

Norman, always happy to intimidate people who were afraid of him, almost seemed to have a grin on his lizardy mouth as he sauntered out of the cage and fixed Jenny with an oddly birdlike upward stare.

"Now, Norman," Jenny coaxed, backing away, "let's not look at me that way."

"He's a..." Danetta began.

"...vegetarian," Jenny finished for her. "Explain to him what a vegetarian *is* while I pour the coffee."

They drank black coffee and Danetta said nothing for several minutes.

"Why are you back?" she asked Jenny. "And what kind of plan do Eugene and...and Cabe—" she almost choked on his name "—have in mind?"

"A really good one, pet," Jenny told her, leaning forward, her soft blond hair dancing around her shoulders as she moved. "We're going to plant some information and let the bad guys act on it. You see, what we think they wanted in here when they tore the place up was my map of the strategic metals vein we think we've found."

"The map!" Danetta sat straight up. "But how did they know about it?"

"You told them."

"Now wait a minute, I only mentioned it to Ben," the younger woman began, and then flushed. "Oh, no, he wouldn't!"

"Oh, yes, he would," she was assured. "Haven't you noticed that he drives a Jaguar? Think about it, you must know what Cabe's executives get paid."

"I never connected it. Ben, mixed up in theft?"

"Ben didn't do it," Jenny told her. "He doesn't even really know what he's into. He's been told that he's helping to find a new oil field, and he's being well paid for digging out information about it. He has no idea that foreign agents are involved."

"How can foreign agents get their hands on metals in this country?" Danetta wanted to know.

"Pet, you can't be that naive," Jenny said gently. "Haven't you ever heard of foreign investors? All they have to do is quickly buy up the land we're prospecting on."

"Can't you do it first?"

"It's not profitable to buy land on speculation, especially this kind of land. Even to bid on it would arouse comment, because it's apparently just scrub. People might not catch on that we had mining interests in it, but they might suspect that we wanted it for a nuclear waste dump or something, and we'd be backed against the wall overnight.''

"Now I understand," Danetta replied. "Well, what are we going to do about Ben?''

"You're going to give him some information when he comes back next Friday from his sales trip.''

Danetta hadn't even thought about the long week ahead, when she'd have to see Cabe every day, have to face him after what they'd done together. Her hands gripped the coffee cup like a lifeline. How was she going to bear it?

"Then what, after I tell Ben?" she asked Jenny.

"We wait for results," Jenny replied. "Remember hearing Eugene talk about Mr. Hunter?''

"I get cold chills remembering what Eugene mentioned about Mr. Hunter," Danetta replied. "He's some sort of top-level troubleshooter in the organization. He actually mounted a commando raid on one of their offshore rigs in the North Atlantic when it was attacked by terrorists.''

Jenny nodded. "He came back with some nasty scars, but he's a hard man to kill. Anyway, he's going to be on the front line when we set this up.''

"Do we get to meet him?" Danetta asked, all eyes.

Jenny shifted restlessly. "I've already met him," she said with uncharacteristic discomfort. "He hates me, in fact.''

"What did you do to him?''

"Nothing, that's the puzzling thing. I guess I remind him of somebody, or maybe he just hates blondes. He seems to be the soul of courtesy with everybody else. You'll probably like him.''

"I like most people," Danetta sighed. She sipped her coffee.

"Why are you home alone? I thought you were staying with the Ritters.''

Danetta blushed furiously.

"Another run-in with the boss?" Jenny asked with pursed lips. "Oh, Dina, what am I going to do with you?"

"Help me find a new job," Danetta said. "Because I'm going to need one. I can't work for that . . . that womanizer another day!"

"So he finally made a pass, huh?" Jenny grinned at the other girl's discomfort, blissfully ignorant of what had really happened. "You can't blame him. He's ruggedly masculine and you're a pretty little thing. I expect your innocence was like a breath of spring to him."

That was very likely true, but it hurt to hear it.

"What's that?" Jenny asked, frowning as she listened.

Danetta heard it, too. Loud, furious footsteps that came to a sudden stop just outside the apartment, followed by angry muttering and a fierce knock on the door.

"I'll give you two guesses who that is," Jenny said sweetly and got up to answer it.

Cabe didn't even bother with a formal greeting. His blue eyes were shooting sparks. He looked very Western in jeans and a freshly pressed chambray shirt, and a black Stetson on his thick hair. "Where is she?" he asked hotly.

Jenny had good instincts. She stepped aside. "She's in the kitchen with the giant lizard," she informed him.

He stormed in, his footsteps as furious as the expression on his broad, dark face. And for once, he didn't even notice Norman, who was doing his spitting-cat imitation with great finesse. Cabe walked right past him without a downward glance. So Norman relaxed his dewlap and went to sleep.

Danetta resisted the urge to jump up and run. She sat very still, gripping her coffee cup, her soft gray eyes looking up at Cabe with pure anguish.

He started to demand an explanation. Then he saw that tearful expression, that wounded look, and every last bit of anger went out of him in one long sigh.

"Oh, honey," he said softly. "I'm so sorry."

She burst into tears, and he went down on one knee in front of her, gathering her head gently onto his broad shoulder, his hands tender in her unruly hair.

"Now, now," he murmured. "It's all right."

"No, it's...not," she hiccuped. Her hands wrapped around his strong neck and she buried her face in his shirt. It smelled of fabric softener and cologne, the spicy scent he always wore, and it was heaven to have him close and warm and not hating her.

He stroked her hair with his hand, noticing that Jenny had discreetly removed herself from the room and closed the door. He wondered what, if anything, Danetta had told her.

"Why did you run away?" he asked her.

"You know."

"No, I don't." He forced her wet face out into the open and looked into her red-rimmed, drowning gray eyes. Rain gray, he thought, or doves-wing gray. So pretty. "Or maybe I do," he amended quietly, and his face grew solemn. "I didn't mean to give you the idea that I took what we did together for granted. I was upset."

She lowered her eyes to his hard mouth. "So was I," she said. She traced his collar idly. "I've never done anything like, well, like...that...before. I thought you were sorry about it, that you'd just wanted me and then when it was over, you wanted to get away from me." She shifted in his embrace. "I thought maybe you'd feel better about things if I just left quietly, without a fuss."

He drew in a long, slow breath and his eyes closed. "You don't understand. I don't know how to make you understand what I felt. I'm thirty-six, and in all my life, all my encounters with women, I've always been in control. Then last night I let it get out of hand deliberately, and with a virgin, of all people. I was ashamed of what I'd done. Guilty. Maybe a little afraid," he added tersely. "That much emotion is a bit unsettling."

She bit her lower lip, staring over his shoulder at the wall. Wasn't he saying that he regretted what had happened?

"Well, you don't have to worry," she said with quiet pride. "I won't embarrass you or anything...."

He drew back, searching her soft eyes. His thumb came up to wipe the tears away while he chose his words very carefully. "I'm not embarrassed," he said softly. He managed a tender smile. "But I think you are."

She blushed, remembering the way it had been, the feverish need, the expression on his hard face when his body had convulsed with pleasure. She dropped her eyes with a little gasp.

He caught her hand in his and brought its soft palm to his mouth. "Don't be shy," he said, leaning forward to nuzzle his face against hers. "I don't have any intention of making suggestive remarks or teasing you about what happened. It isn't the kind of thing a man makes light of."

That gave her enough courage to lift her eyes. She'd been terrified that he was going to make fun of her embarrassment. But he wasn't smiling, although there was a soft, quiet glow in his pale blue eyes.

"You missed breakfast," he said gently. "Want to go somewhere with me and have waffles?"

She hesitated. "I can't leave Jenny."

"Then suppose we make some waffles."

She blinked away the rest of her tears and wiped her wet eyes. "Cabe, I don't have a waffle iron."

He gave her an exasperated stare. "No waffle iron? What am I supposed to live on, if you can't make me waffles?"

She felt and looked thoroughly confused. She lifted a slender hand to push back her long, light brown hair. "I can make pancakes," she faltered.

"I like waffles," he said firmly. "I do not like liver and onions or turnips, so don't ever fix them. I like my coffee black and strong, and I'm partial to spaghetti, rare steak, macaroni and cheese casserole and fried ocean perch, and apple and peach pies."

This was getting confusing. Her gray eyes searched his. "Do you want them all right now?" she asked.

"I'm just listing the most important things," he explained. "Later we can go into specifics, like how I do not like my eggs cooked. Oh, and don't ever make quiche because I read in this book that real men don't eat it." He grinned.

She felt a smile tickling her mouth and gave in to it. She'd never known him like this. "Okay."

His chest swelled with pure delight as he looked at her. It was going to be all right after all. He could win her over, if he worked at it very carefully. But he had to pace it right. He couldn't rush her, or move too fast. He'd already made one big mistake by letting things go too far last night. Now he had to prove to her that it wasn't just physical with him. He had to reassure her that his emotions were every bit as involved as his body. Waking up and finding her gone this morning had terrified him to his very bones. He'd been cold with the fear that she might mean to disappear where he couldn't find her. And here she sat, waiting. Sort of.

"Meanwhile," he said, "we'll go out and get some waffles. Jenny can come, too. Why don't you go and get her."

"I could fix us something here," she tried again.

"Honey, I'm dying for a waffle," he sighed.

She gave in. "I'll just find a sweater. I hadn't unpacked."

His eyes went to her suitcase and back to her wan expression in time to see the faint glint of fear in her face. "It's all right," he said quietly. His hand brushed over her cheek lightly. "Don't be afraid. We won't go over the line again, I promise."

She swallowed. "What do you want?" she asked because she had to know.

"You," he said simply.

"But you . . ."

"But I what?" he asked, his voice deep and slow and velvety soft. "But I had you, is that what you're trying to say?" He smiled gently. "I jumped the gun and almost ruined everything, but I want to start again. This time, I'll get it in the right order."

She looked up at him in total confusion.

"We'll take it one day at a time," he said. "We'll go places together, I'll send you flowers and candy, I'll call you at two in the morning just to talk, and we'll make love— although," he added ruefully, "we won't let it go all the way again. Not until we know each other well enough."

"And then?"

He took her by the shoulders and shook her gently. "And then, what do you think? That I'll drag you back to my place and make love to you until you can't walk for three days? God knows, it's what I'd like to do right now. But I'm willing to wait until you're ready for that, until you understand that I'm not trying to make you into one of my Saturday-night specials."

"In other words," she said, fighting tears again, "you want me to be your mistress."

His thumbs grew idly caressing on her upper arms and he studied her for a long moment. "Why is it so difficult for you to believe that I could want you permanently? I told you long ago that I wasn't a playboy."

"You told me a long time ago that you didn't want commitment or love," she added.

"That was before," he said doggedly.

"Before I went crazy in the garage and wound up like a straight pin in your conscience," she said.

He let her go, exasperated. "You won't listen!"

"You just feel guilty and I know it," she mumbled, turning away from him. "You won't get around me by telling me fairy stories."

"No? I've got some great ideas for a version of Red Riding Hood," he muttered, his eyes narrowing on her straight back.

"Pervert!" she threw at him.

His eyebrows arched. "What?"

"An elderly lady and a furry wolf, what would you call it!"

"I had in mind Red and the wolf, honey," he murmured dryly, "and you've got the animal part just about right."

"You stay away from me," she threatened. "I won't let you change my mind. I'm going to find another job."

"No, you aren't," he said with a wry smile. "If I have to give you a reference, I'll tell them all that you carry a submachine gun in your purse and you're part of a counterfeit car ring."

"Nobody will believe you."

"Your uncle will," he reminded her. "You know, the one who thinks I manufacture photon torpedoes . . . ?"

She backed to the wall. "Norman!" she called to the giant lizard as a last resort.

Norman cocked an eye at her and closed it immediately.

"Turncoat!" she muttered.

"He likes me," Cabe told her. "I didn't back away from him, so now he respects me. We're going to be great buddies." He glanced down at the reptile uncomfortably and one eye narrowed. "Well, maybe distant buddies," he amended.

"I can't work for you anymore," she tried again.

He shrugged. "I'll agree with that. You're going to have your work cut out at home."

She frowned. "What do you mean, at home?"

He stared pointedly at her stomach and pursed his lips. "Can you knit?"

Her mouth opened as she tried to find something to say. She couldn't believe he'd said what she thought she heard.

"Is it okay to come out now?" Jenny called from the hall. "I've only just gotten to the apartment and I'm starved."

"We were just talking about food," Cabe lied glibly, turning with easy courtesy. "Get your sweater and we'll all go to that nice little chain-store breakfast place and stuff ourselves on pecan waffles."

Danetta escaped past him, so confused and unsettled that it took her ages to fix her face and find a sweater. She didn't know what had gotten into Cabe Ritter, but whatever it was, she had a feeling that she was going to be on the run.

And so she was. It didn't stop at breakfast. He was back for supper, charming Cousin Jenny but never flirting or making eyes at her. He treated her as if she were one of his own relations, and his attitude toward Danetta turned warm and protective without any sexual undercurrents at all.

The next day, his behavior at the office followed the pattern he'd set the day before. He opened doors for her, took her sweater, brought her coffee, and generally treated her like his own lady.

She was halfway between heaven and earth, so shocked at the change that she messed up half the letters as she typed them and had to do them over again.

But the real shocker came when Karol stopped by the office and demanded to see Cabe.

Danetta buzzed him, but instead of having Karol come in, he came out.

"There you are, darling, your little petunia here wasn't very forthcoming," Karol murmured sweetly, settling her body as close to his as she could get it. "Are we going dancing tonight?"

"Sorry, honey, I'm off the market as of Saturday," he said with a pleasant smile. "Danetta and I are going to Big Tom's for supper and then I'm taking her to meet an uncle of mine who lives in West Tulsa."

Karol stared at him blankly while the words sank in. "You're taking your secretary out on a date?" she asked.

Danetta was sure she looked as stunned as Karol did, especially when Cabe glanced at her with a smile that could have taken rust off a waterlogged iron skillet.

"That's right," Cabe replied.

"Why?" Karol demanded.

"To get the family used to her, for one thing," he said, deliberately obtuse. "My dad and my stepmother like her, and my brother's crazy about her already. We had a great weekend out at Dad's ranch."

"So that's where you were," Karol said icily. "Well, don't expect me to stand around waiting while you take this child out on dates. I've got better things to do with my time!"

"Glad to hear it," Cabe agreed with a smile. "Why don't you go and do some of them?"

Karol gave him a furious glare and stormed out of the office.

Cabe brushed his hands together. "So much for that complication." He turned to Danetta. "Better reserve us a table at Big Tom's," he said. "And wear something bright for Uncle Abe. You'll like him. He used to be a Texas Ranger, and he can tell some tales!''

"You meant all that you told her?" Danetta asked.

"Sure I did." He frowned, sticking his hands into his pockets. "You don't get it, do you? I'm serious. No more women for window dressing, no more all-night poker games with my old cronies, no more long trips out of town. I'm settling down. Not that I expect you to believe me without some proof, so you can see for yourself as we go along that I mean it."

Her heart was doing a wild dance number in her chest. "All this... is for me?" she asked shyly.

"Not for anyone else I know," he said, smiling. "You're pretty when you smile like that. You warm my heart."

She blushed, touched by the softness of his deep voice, by the flowery words. Probably he'd said these things before, but they sounded genuine to Danetta.

"Make the reservation," he said gently. "What kind of flowers do you like, by the way?"

"Daisies," she replied.

"I thought so." He went back into his office without another word.

That night she had a corsage of daisies to wear on her dress. They ate at Big Tom's and then went to see Cabe's Uncle Abe, who seemed to enjoy the visit as much as Danetta did.

"He's delightful," she told Cabe when they drove home in a misting rain.

"I love the old rascal, although most of the family can't take him in large doses." He glanced at her. She looked lovely in her black cocktail dress with the daisies at her breast on the lacy jacket that covered the spaghetti straps. "I thought you might like him." He put his cigarette to his lips and took a long draw. "But then, you like everybody, don't you, honey?"

"Most people," she said. "Some are hard to like. You have to look under the surface sometimes to find the warm places."

"Does the green lizard really have a warm place?"

"The books all say that lizards aren't affectionate, and some books say that iguanas are stupid." She shrugged and smiled to herself. "Maybe they're right, but Norman listens to me when I talk to him, and he comes when I whistle, and just occasionally he does actually seem to understand what I say. I don't know if it's intelligence or instinct, but he's different with most people than he is with me."

"He liked Nicky."

"Oh, so did I," she said.

He put out the cigarette as they wound down Tulsa's city streets on the way to her apartment, the bright lights looking cozy and intimate in the rain and the darkness of night. "I never gave Nicky a chance. Or Cynthia, either, for that matter. But Dad and I had a long talk yesterday, and I'm only beginning to see what a fool I was. Nicky deserves more attention than I gave him. Fortunately he's still young enough not to hold grudges. I plan to make up for my attitude." He pulled the Lincoln up in front of her building and cut off the lights and the engine. "He could stay with us once in a while, if you wouldn't mind."

Her breath rustled in her throat. "Stay with us?" she echoed blankly, and her eyes turned to Cabe's in the dim streetlight's glow.

He reached out and touched her cheek, drawing his fingers warmly down it to her soft mouth. "With us."

She swallowed as he unfastened her seat belt, and his own, and drew her gently to him. "You mean, we're going to live together?" she faltered as his warm mouth brushed lazily against her own.

"Married people usually do. Yes, that's it, open your mouth..."

She did, trying to speak, but he had another entirely different function in mind. She felt his tongue darting past her lips and the lights went out. She could refuse him nothing once he touched her. Her arms went around him almost convulsively and her mouth answered his, a soft moan working its way out of her throat as the fever burned high and bright. His hands had moved from her thighs to her breasts, searching for fastenings before he suddenly came to his senses and realized where they were.

"What an incredibly stupid thing to do," he ground out, wrapping her up tight and shuddering as his face slid down into her warm throat. "Hold tight," he whispered, feeling his trembling reflected in her own soft body. "Just hold tight until we stop shaking."

She lay against him struggling for breath, while her mind tried to absorb what he'd said before he kissed her. "You said... married people," she murmured.

"That's right." He nuzzled his cheek against hers. "What do you think?"

She pulled away from him. "I think it would be better if you were sure," she replied, looking into his intent eyes bravely.

"You don't think I am?"

She smiled. "No. You've been free for a long time. And what happened at your father's ranch, well, it happened quickly. I might not be pregnant," she added nervously.

He shrugged. "Then we'll try again," he said. "After we're married," he emphasized, tapping her gently on the tip of the nose. "No more messing around on couches."

"But aren't you asking me to marry you because I could be pregnant?" she asked.

"No."

"Because I was a virgin," she persisted.

"No."

"Then why?"

He bent and kissed her, very gently. "When you work it out, you can come and tell me. Let's go up. Jenny will worry."

She waited until he opened the door for her, and he walked her to the elevator and out to her apartment. He kissed her good-night, a bare brush of his lips over hers, gave her a warm smile and walked away whistling. Danetta went into the apartment no wiser than when she'd left.

Eleven

The rest of the week went by in a flash. Cabe took Danetta out every night, but there were no more passionate kisses in his car—or anywhere else for that matter. He held hands with her, his grip faintly possessive, his eyes exquisitely tender as he looked down at her. He never mentioned Karol, and she didn't call him. It was just as he'd said: he was closing the door on the past.

Jenny marveled at the reformed playboy, not realizing that it had all been an act on his part. Danetta didn't enlighten her, either. She was too much in love and too overwhelmed with Cabe's attentiveness to bother with explanations. She was praying that their new relationship would last.

He never talked to her about the night in the garage. He never referred to it again, although once in a while she couldn't help but notice the way his eyes wandered to her flat belly and lingered there with an odd glow in them. But his conduct was above reproach, in public and in private.

Friday came, and Cabe drew Danetta into his office, closing the door quietly behind them.

"Ben just came in," he told her. "He'll ask you out to lunch if we're right about him. You have to accept."

She searched his hard eyes. "You don't want me to."

"No," he said with husky possession in his voice. "But I have to let you. Everything depends on it. We're baiting a trap. In this case, it's necessary. These men are dangerous. It was a burglary at first, but it might get more deadly as we go along. We have to stop them, now."

She felt a twinge of fear, but she smiled in spite of it. "Okay."

His hand slid into her hair and he pulled her cheek to his broad chest, holding her gently while he stared over her head and wondered how he could trust her to a reprehensible man like Ben. If anything happened to her, he'd never be able to live with it.

"You be careful," he said above her head. "If you feel afraid at all, for any reason, get away from him and call me. I won't leave the office."

"He won't hurt me," she said, portraying more confidence than she felt. She drew back and lifted soft, caring eyes to his. "Don't worry."

"How can I help it?" he asked quietly. "You're my life."

She caught her breath and tears burned her eyes as she saw the fierce possessiveness in his face. "I'll be very, very careful," she promised.

He laughed coldly. "Don't take chances. Don't go anywhere alone with him. Anywhere, even to a phone booth, do you understand me?"

"You're bristling with chauvinism, Mr. Ritter," she said demurely.

"That, bad temper and hunger," he added curtly.

"I can't do anything about the chauvinism and bad temper," she murmured, sliding her arms slowly around his strong neck, feeling confident and possessive herself for the first time. "But I think I can take care of the hunger part," she breathed as she drew his mouth down over hers.

For a long moment he just stood there. Then a sound broke from his lips, a smothered kind of groan, and his arms enveloped her, gently lifting her so that she fit against his tall frame. He kissed her with devouring ardor, so lost in her that he wouldn't have heard a bomb go off at the door.

"My mistake," she said seconds later when they were both shivering. "I think I just made it worse!"

"You're going to have to marry me," he ground out against her mouth. "Think up any excuse you like—possible pregnancy, guilty conscience—whatever will get you to the altar. But it has to be soon. My God, I'm starving to death!"

She felt the shudder run through him and her eyes opened, soft like gray down, ardent. "We could lock the door," she suggested hesitantly.

"No. Once on a sofa was more than enough," he said stiffly. He brushed his mouth over her cheekbone and down to her lips. "I should have been stronger, for your sake. I should have held back."

"It's all right," she whispered, shocked at the emotion in his deep voice.

"It damned well is not," he said tersely. He lifted his head to look at her. "You deserved a white wedding with all the trimmings, right down to a respectable wedding night. I cheated you out of it, and I'm sorry."

She didn't know what to say. She hadn't expected that kind of regret, or such a statement from a man like Cabe. "Do I really know you at all?" she asked softly.

"Not very well," he admitted. "But I'm working on it. The white wedding you'll get, belatedly. And I promise you, your wedding night is going to be everything it should have been." His eyes searched hers with soft tenderness. "I'll make you believe you're still a virgin."

She colored and leaned her cheek against his. "When you talk to me like this, I feel like one," she whispered.

His arms contracted. "I can't regret the pleasure," he whispered huskily. "I've remembered it at night, sometimes, and I'd have to get up and go for a walk just to relax. The need was white hot. It still is. But it's not just physical," he added, searching for words. "It's a wholeness. A oneness. I told you that night that I felt as if I'd been shaken to the core of my soul. That's what it was like. Shattering and humbling. Reverent." His eyes closed.

With a wild little cry she buried her face in his throat, shivering all over with shocked pleasure. At the time she'd felt like that, too, but she'd convinced herself that he only felt guilty. Now she knew better. It was so sweet. Like being given the key to a candy store at the age of six. Like walking on air. Tears washed down her face and she laughed through them.

"You do care, don't you?" she asked brokenly.

"That's a mild way of putting it," he replied on a forced laugh. His eyes were closed and he was rocking her against him. She felt heavenly.

"Say the words," she pleaded, tightening her grip on his neck.

He drew back, though, and shook his head, smiling. "Not yet."

"When?"

"On our wedding night," he said. He pushed back her hair, adoring her face with his eyes. "I'll say it until you're sick of hearing it."

"I never will be," she promised.

He set her back on her feet. "In that case, it's going to be a long night."

She smiled at him. "Promise."

He kissed her eyes closed. "I promise. Now get back out there and accept a date with Ben while I try not to think about how many guns I've got at the apartment."

She moved away from him reluctantly. "Everything will be all right," she said. "Jenny says Eugene's main troubleshooter is going to be in charge tonight."

"Yes, I know." He cocked an eyebrow. "Have you ever met Hunter?"

"No. Jenny says he's...well, rough."

"Rough doesn't cover it." He grinned. "Former Green Beret, former CIA, former mercenary...I guess Hunter's done it all. He pulled our irons out of the fire overseas, and he's still doing it. We place a lot of trust in him on this kind of thing." His face hardened. "I don't envy Ben's colleagues when Hunter gets a hold on them."

"What if Ben doesn't bite the bait?"

"He will," Cabe said grimly.

And he did. Ben invited her to lunch and, under the guise of asking casual questions, managed to get out of her that Jenny had brought all sorts of maps and documents home with her, and that she and Jenny had been invited to a party and would be away from home all evening. Ben deposited her at the office and went off with a thoughtful smile on his face.

"Well?" Cabe prompted when she was in his office with the door closed.

She grinned. "He bit!"

"Hallelujah," he chuckled. "Okay. Get to work. Now we wait."

That night Cabe wore his dinner jacket with a black tie and a faintly ruffled white shirt above well-tailored black slacks. He looked elegant and very, very sexy and Danetta had to grit her teeth to keep from throwing herself at him when he came to pick her up at the apartment.

"You look great," she sighed.

His own eyes were going over her electric-blue satin dress with its low neckline and midcalf skirt. It was close fitting and very elegant, and his smile was predatory. "You dish, you."

"Don't I even rate a mention?" Jenny asked, her hands on her hips. She was wearing a red dress, slit up one side and buttoned to the throat with black satin clasps to hold it together. It shouldn't have suited her fairness, but it did. With her long hair around her shoulders and a minimum of makeup on, she looked devastating.

"Nice color," Cabe remarked.

"I'm living down to the image your colleague has of me," she said haughtily.

Danetta had to hide a giggle. Jenny looked uncharacteristically hostile, and Danetta found herself wondering just how deeply the mysterious Mr. Hunter had gotten under her skin.

She didn't have long to wait. There was a curt knock on the door and Jenny went to open it before Danetta could.

"Good evening," she said in the same tones a judge might use when ordering an execution.

A tall, dark-eyed man came into the room. He was dressed, as Cabe was, in evening clothes, but he had a face as cold and hard as ice, and his thin mouth looked as if it had never smiled. His hair was an echo of his eyes, almost black, and his skin was very dark. He had extremely high cheekbones and a nose as straight as a ruler. Danetta thought at first that he had a vaguely oriental look. Then those dark eyes met hers and she realized that he was Indian. American Indian.

"This is Mr. Hunter," Jenny introduced him without looking at him again. "Danetta Marist," she continued, nodding toward Danetta, "and that's..."

"Hello, Cabe," the newcomer said. His voice was deep and curt, without any inflection or accent.

"Hunter," Cabe replied. "It's been a long time."

The man called Hunter turned back to Jenny. "You, I presume, are my date?"

"You're a big, strong man," Jenny said with a venomous smile. "You ought to be able to survive an evening in my company."

Everyone smiled, except the icy Mr. Hunter. He checked the watch on his wrist. "We'd better go."

"Are we ready?" Cabe asked with a pointed question in the eyes that met Hunter's.

Hunter nodded. "The reservations are confirmed," he said, and let his black eyes slide sideways toward a nearby lamp.

Cabe nodded back. "Then let's go," he said, taking Danetta's arm. "I'm starved!"

They went out together. Danetta noticed that Mr. Hunter stayed on one side of the elevator on the way down and Jenny stayed on the other. It was so obvious as to be amusing that they were going to neutral corners. She wondered what had caused the ice age to move in.

The restaurant was crowded, but they were seated quickly.

"Now what?" Danetta asked.

"Now we wait," Hunter replied. He studied the menu briefly and laid it down, staring around at the glitter of crystal. His eyes made an emphatic statement about his feelings toward it.

"What are you going to have, Jenny?" Danetta asked while she tried to decide between chicken cordon bleu and steak medallions in cheese sauce.

Jenny glanced toward Hunter. "Something raw," she muttered. "Oysters, maybe."

Hunter lifted an eyebrow and glanced down at her. He didn't say a word, but Jenny suddenly blushed and averted her gaze to the menu. "The shrimp creole looks good," she said nervously.

"I want a rare steak," Cabe said. He glanced at Hunter and grinned. "How about you?" He added something gutteral and totally incomprehensible to Danetta and Jenny.

Hunter replied in the same rough-sounding language and a corner of his thin mouth quirked. He added, in English, "But I'll settle for beef."

"What language was that?" Danetta asked, fascinated.

"Apache," Cabe told her. He smiled at her expression. "Didn't I ever tell you that my grandmother was Apache? So was an uncle somewhere back down the line. Grandmother taught me the language. It's easy, once you get the hang of the glottal stops and the long and short sounds of the vowels."

"And once you learn the nuances of inflection that turn an insult into a compliment," Hunter added, a twinkle in the dark eyes that glanced off Cabe's.

"It came in handy once when Hunter and I were in a tight situation overseas," Cabe told Danetta. "We knew our hotel room was bugged, so we spoke in Apache."

"I understand my counterpart thought it was some new American code. He spent the better part of a year trying to break it."

"Did he?" Jenny asked hesitantly, her pale eyes suddenly riveted on his dark face.

He wouldn't look at her. "They killed him before he could. Failure is expensive."

Jenny lifted her water glass and took a long sip. She didn't say another word, and Hunter didn't, either.

Halfway through the meal, they heard a soft beeping sound. Hunter took out a communications device that no one knew he had and spoke into it.

"They've sprung the trap." He got up. "No, stay and enjoy your meal," he said when Cabe started to rise. "This is my party now."

Jenny got to her feet, too. "I assume I'll be needed to identify the gentleman you think was after me?" she asked, but she didn't look up.

"Yes," Hunter said shortly. "And then you can go back to your job and leave the spy game to people who know how to play it."

She glared at him and then turned away abruptly, her lower lip trembling. "Shall we go, Mr. Hunter?" she asked coldly. She managed a smile for Cabe and Danetta. "Good night. I'll see you later, Dina."

Danetta nodded, watching them walk away, careful not to even touch each other.

"Talk about the cold war," she mused, her eyes following them.

"They've been enemies since they met. God knows why, they look like two halves of a whole, despite the differences in size and coloring." He reached over and took her hand. "Name a date."

She stared down at his big hand. "Do you mean it?"

He smiled. "With all my heart."

"May the fifth," she said.

His eyebrows lifted. "Why?"

"Because I like to say *cinco de mayo*?" she suggested.

He shook his head. "Okay. Suit yourself. Tomorrow, you go and buy a wedding gown. How about a honeymoon in Jamaica?"

She gasped. "Oh, could we!"

"You bet."

She smiled at him with her heart in her eyes. Then the smile faded. "Cabe, we can't go to Jamaica!"

"Why not?" he asked.

"Norman!"

He pursed his lips amusedly. "Now I've got a great idea about a vacation for Norman. There's a big jungle down in South America..."

"Iguanas don't take vacations to South America," she said.

"In that case, suppose we let Nicky keep him?"

She laughed. "That would delight both of them."

And, in fact, it did. A week later, the enemy agents were in safe hands, Ben Meadows was unemployed and facing charges of conspiracy, Jenny was back to work for Eugene after the wedding, and Cabe and Danetta were languishing on a deserted moonlit white sand beach near Montego Bay on a private estate that Cabe had rented for the occasion.

"It's heavenly," Danetta sighed, lying against Cabe without a stitch on her body, her cheek on Cabe's bare chest.

"So are you, honey," he smiled, bending to kiss her lazily. The three days they'd been here had gone by all too rapidly. He looked down the length of her body in the moonlight, wondering at the delight of making love to her. It had been, as he promised, like the first time all over again. Now he was teaching her new things, new ways of arousal that made them both dizzy with pleasure.

"Are you sure nobody will see us?" she asked. They'd just been in swimming, and he'd insisted that it was the experience of a lifetime without clothing in the moonlight. It had been. Now they were stretched out on two enormous beach towels laid overlapping in the sand, and he was looking at her with an expression that was just a little cooler than the warm winds.

"Nobody will see us," he murmured. His lips touched her breasts, making them peak, and slowly he drew her against and then over him, so that they were touching all the way up and down.

"How can it be so sweet every time?" she whispered when his hands slid down her hips and began to move them in sensuous patterns against his own.

"Because we love each other," he whispered back, smiling as he nibbled her lips. "Are you tired of hearing it, yet?"

"Oh, no," she sighed into his mouth.

"I love you," he murmured. His hands moved her again, and this time he shifted so that she became part of him with one smooth motion.

She gasped, feeling him merge with her, biting his chest in her shocked pleasure. "Cabe," she whispered jerkily.

"Sit up."

"I can't!" she exclaimed, all nerves and shy fright.

"Yes, you can. I'm your husband and I love you, and you love me. We're married. Do it."

He coaxed her with his hands and hips until finally she did what he wanted her to do. He held her hips, watching her with a warm, wicked smile until the silky movement began to make his tension swiftly unbearable.

"That's it," he murmured, his hands biting into her hips as he guided her. He laughed through his building anguish.

Her own body was shaking, and she felt the sounds building in her throat as the pleasure grew until she bit off a cry.

"Let me hear you," he said huskily. "No one else is going to. Is it good?"

"Yes," she cried. "Oh, yes...!"

He jerked her body down in an agony of need. He was shaking all over, his hands hurting her hips in their ardent need, his back arching.

"Look at me!" he whispered roughly.

She did, her body fluid above his. Harsh moans burst from his lips as he held her in place, his eyes holding hers in rapt fascination.

She felt his completion before she saw it take him, and for the first time, she watched. It was so erotic that her own body quickly began to tauten and she sobbed helplessly, clinging to him. He barely took time to get his breath before he whipped her over onto her back with raging hunger and began all over again the hard, exquisite motions until she was shivering and crying with her own satisfaction.

She lay in his arms drowned in sweat, overcome by the oneness. It never ceased to amaze her that two people could be so close.

He stroked her hair, his lips traveling gently all over her face, tenderly calming her.

"You watched me this time," he whispered at her ear. "It doesn't embarrass you so much now, does it?"

"Not as much as it did at the beginning," she confessed. She nuzzled her face against his hairy chest. "Cabe, I think I may be pregnant," she whispered.

He smiled at her temple. "I know."

She searched his gentle eyes. "Do you mind?" she asked, smiling back at him.

"Not at all." He kissed her tenderly. "Do you?"

"No. I'm rather looking forward to it." She nibbled his lower lip. "What are we going to do about Norman?"

"Let Nicky adopt him," he suggested. "Then you can visit him whenever you like."

"All right," she agreed finally. She was going to miss Norman. Of course an iguana wasn't quite the companion Cabe was. She'd have to think of it that way.

He sensed her faint sadness. "I'll compromise. Later, if we have a boy, we might get him a baby one to raise. Of course," he added darkly, "he will be my son, and he may not like lizards at all."

"That's true," she agreed easily, averting her wicked smile. "He may just looove snakes . . . oh!"

He jerked her back down and kissed her breathless.

The winds from the sea blew softly over them. Danetta closed her eyes and sighed happily. Her own small corner of island and the only man in the world she loved. She smiled, thinking that this willingly beached couple were rewriting *Robinson Crusoe* with a girl Friday instead of a boy. As her gaze settled on Cabe's dark face, she decided that his girl Friday was what she most wanted to be. She closed her eyes and settled into Cabe's arms to drink in the moonlight. And the world seemed a very long way away.

*   *   *   *   *

SILHOUETTE *Desire*®

COMING NEXT MONTH

#529 SHILOH'S PROMISE—BJ James
November's *Man of the Month*, Shiloh Butler, was a dark, brooding man. He'd sworn to protect his friend's widow, Megan Sullivan, from danger—but who would protect her from him?

#530 INTERLUDE—Donna Carlisle
A Rocky Mountain blizzard forced wealthy adventurer Alan Donovan and practical schoolteacher Pamela Mercer into close contact.
Though they were dependent on each other for survival, surely *these* two opposites couldn't attract.

#531 ULTERIOR MOTIVES—Laura Leone
Ross Tanner looked awfully good to Shelley Baird. He was suave, charming and debonair. But that was before she realized he worked for her language school's major rival!

#532 BLUE CHIP BRIDE—Audra Adams
If Janet Demarest married Ken Radnor, he'd get her stock, she'd get her money, and then they'd get the marriage annulled.
Simple...until Ken decided he wanted a great deal more....

#533 SEEING IS BELIEVING—Janet Bieber
Optometrist Lynda Fisher was far too busy for romance—especially with someone like Kent Berringer. But when she opened her eyes she realized that Mr. Wrong was actually Mr. Right!

#534 TAGGED—Lass Small
Another Lambert meets her match. For Fredricka Lambert, Colin Kilgallon had always been just a good friend. But lately, he'd given a whole new meaning to the word "friendship."

AVAILABLE NOW:

#523 BRANIGAN'S TOUCH
Leslie Davis Guccione

#524 WITH A LITTLE SPICE
Sara Chance

#525 A PACKAGE DEAL
Ariel Berk

#526 BEFORE DAWN
Terry Lawrence

#527 ADDED DELIGHT
Mary Lynn Baxter

#528 HIS GIRL FRIDAY
Diana Palmer

⚜ SILHOUETTE®
Desire™

ANOTHER BRIDE FOR A BRANIGAN BROTHER!

Branigan's Touch
by Leslie Davis Guccione

Available in October 1989

You've written in asking for more about the Branigan brothers, so we decided to give you Jody's story—from *his* perspective.

Look for Mr. October—*Branigan's Touch*—a *Man of the Month*, coming from Silhouette Desire.

Following #311 *Bittersweet Harvest*, #353 *Still Waters* and #376 *Something in Common*, *Branigan's Touch* still stands on its own. You'll enjoy the warmth and charm of the Branigan clan— and watch the sparks fly when another Branigan man meets his match with an O'Connor woman!

SD523-1

READERS' COMMENTS ON SILHOUETTE DESIRES

"Thank you for Silhouette Desires. They are the best thing that has happened to the bookshelves in a long time."
—V.W.*, Knoxville, TN

"Silhouette Desires—wonderful, fantastic—the best romance around."
—H.T.*, Margate, N.J.

"As a writer as well as a reader of romantic fiction, I found DESIREs most refreshingly realistic—and definitely as magical as the love captured on their pages."
—C.M.*, Silver Lake, N.Y.

"I just wanted to let you know how very much I enjoy your Silhouette Desire books. I read other romances, and I must say your books rate up at the top of the list."
—C.N.*, Anaheim, CA

"Desires are number one. I especially enjoy the endings because they just don't leave you with a kiss or embrace; they finish the story. Thank you for giving me such reading pleasure."
—M.S.*, Sandford, FL

*names available on request